"Get tough, Casey! A good reporter has to get tough!"

Ben Steele's advice echoed in her head as Casey raced across the courthouse grounds in pursuit of the tall figure retreating down the back steps.

"Mr. Simpson! Wait!" she called, gulping for breath.

The desperation in her voice spun him around again, the eyes blue stones now, chipping away at her self-confidence as he glared down at her diminutive frame as though she were a small yapping puppy obstructing his path.

There was only one sure way to gain his attention. She had to try it.

"Mr. Simpson!" Her voice was commanding; her tone, firm and authoritative. "How do you think losing this important case will affect your reputation as a winning attorney?"

The question directed upward to the rock-hard jaw had scarcely left her lips when he wheeled around with a cold fury that rocked her back on her heels.

"Obviously, I'm *not* a winning attorney," he growled. "I've just been informed that I'm a *lousy* attorney; that any decent lawyer would have won the case." The blue eyes darkened in wounded pride; the rich voice faltered.

"Now you've got your statement," he said wearily, the very life drained from his words. "Are you satisfied?"

A MOUNTAIN TO STAND STRONG

Peggy Darty

Serenade/Serenata
BOOKS

of the Zondervan Publishing House
Grand Rapids, Michigan

A MOUNTAIN TO STAND STRONG
Copyright © 1984 by The Zondervan Corporation
1415 Lake Drive, S.E.
Grand Rapids, Michigan 49506

ISBN 0-310-46532-x

Edited by Anne Severance
Designed by Kim Koning

Printed in the United States of America

   85   86   87   88   89   90   /   10   9   8   7   6   5   4   3   2

To Landon,
who has shared the mountains
and the valleys

CHAPTER 1

"THE JURY HAS reached a verdict!"

Ben Steele's announcement paralyzed the entire WJAK newsroom. Even the telephones stopped ringing momentarily, as if poised for the outcome all Colorado Springs had been awaiting.

The controversial trial had stretched on for weeks, while the city buzzed with speculation. Was the bachelor son of a prominent local family really a diamond thief, or was he merely a pawn in an elaborate game? Attorney Steve Simpson had provided a brilliant defense, disputing the prosecution's evidence and hammering away at damaging testimonies. The fact that Simpson rarely lost a case made the outcome even more interesting.

"Well, tell us!" Casey Green leapt to her feet, unable to contain her curiosity another moment. All eyes shot across the television newsroom to the petite woman who was flicking a strand of tawny blond hair over her shoulder. The tailored navy dress she was wearing further minimized her five-three frame.

Ignoring the stares, Casey's gold-flecked brown eyes widened on the news director's face, imploring him to answer.

"Guil-ty!"

His reply stunned the captive audience. Then suddenly everyone was talking at once. Ben bounded across the room to Casey's desk, his eyes surveying her thoughtfully.

"Take Crew Three and get over there." He raked a nervous hand through his thinning dark hair. "There's another crew inside the courthouse getting interviews. Just try to get the reaction of the man on the street. And hurry!"

"Right." Casey reached under the desk for her tote bag, then hesitated. "Thanks, Ben," she added quickly, ignoring the envious gazes of other reporters as she grabbed her coat and made a dash for the back door, her bag swinging from her shoulder.

"She doesn't know how to walk fast," someone observed. "She always goes at a trot."

"Maybe that's why *she* gets the stories," came the caustic reply.

The words echoed in Casey's ears as she reached the corridor, tossing a doubtful glance toward the closed doors of the elevator, then opting for the stairway instead.

"I get the stories because I work harder," she mumbled, flying down three flights of steps and pushing the back door open. She blinked into the sudden glare of a noonday sun as she headed across the parking lot, the brisk September air cooling her warm cheeks.

In the distance, the motor was already warming on the WJAK van, while big Coy Wilkens stood loading his camera and John Deevers worried over the sound equipment.

An amused grin tilted the corners of Casey's pert

mouth as she regarded the two men, so different in size and temperament, yet perfectly paired to orchestrate camera and sound into successful news coverage.

"Ready?" Coy's deep voice rumbled over the parked cars, hazel eyes widening in his heavily bearded face.

"Guilty—can you believe it?" mused Casey as she trotted across to the van, her gaze flicking absently over the huge man, his arms bare beneath the short sleeved shirt. He always maintained he could work better in short sleeves, even in December, and chose to dispense with heavy coats, as well.

"The whole town has gone wild!" John informed her, folding trailing wires into the back seat. The smaller man, in contrast, was bundled to the chin in heavy parka and cap.

"Let's hurry!" Casey climbed into the van. "But of course I don't have to tell *you* to hurry." The gold flecks danced in her brown eyes as she glanced mischievously at Coy.

"And no one has to tell *you* how to talk," Coy retorted, cranking the engine of the van and roaring out of the parking lot.

"As long as she looks good on the tube, no one cares." John hung over the seat. "Incidentally, you'd better brush your hair, 'Cheryl'!"

While John and a few others had argued her resemblance to Cheryl Ladd, Casey never flattered herself into believing it.

"Give me time, John," she glanced over her shoulder, smiling. "I've had less than five minutes to grab my purse and make a mad dash to the parking lot!"

As the men chuckled, Casey flipped the visor mirror down, examining her reflection critically. Her gaze lingered indifferently on wide-set eyes, sharply arched brows, rosy lips, and a complexion the shade of warm honey. Thick golden hair fell about her small face in total disarray.

She frowned, oblivious to the striking natural beauty that so captivated her television audience. Flipping the mirror back, Casey reached for her tote bag. She had always been concerned with achieving a more enduring beauty and, indeed, she had succeeded, if one tuned in her nightly on-the-street interviews where the camera captured her intense love and compassion for people—people of every age, race, and creed.

"Now where's my hairbrush?" she mumbled, diving into her enormous canvas bag. The jumble of contents within brought an impatient sigh, and she quickly tossed the bag on its side, dragging out the items in search of the elusive brush. A strange mixture composed of pens, pads, random notes, a make-up kit, a small box of raisins and finally a worn New Testament tumbled haphazardly onto the seat.

"Uh-oh," Coy glanced back at John, "she's gonna try to convert us!"

Casey looked up, puzzled, then catching Coy's eyes on her Bible, she grinned back. "Not right now, but I'd better get busy. The way *you* drive, I may not get many more chances."

Laughter rumbled from the broad chest, and he accelerated even more, delighted by her squeal of fear.

She glanced at the buildings zipping by, then forced herself to concentrate again on her hair. Plucking a comb from the make-up kit, she dragged it through the thick cloud of hair swirling about her shoulders.

"Guess I forgot my brush," she said under her breath, flipping back through her possessions to retrieve a colorful headband, which she clamped over her rebellious hair in quick dismissal.

With her hair swept back, the classic bone structure of Casey's face was enhanced, giving her a younger, more vulnerable quality than her twenty-four years should have allowed.

She turned to the items strewn over the front seat, dashing everything back into her tote bag. Her slim fingers lingered on the soft leather of her New Testament, her brown eyes warmly reflective.

While Coy often teased her about her religious beliefs, she wondered how he and John, like so many others, could face life without the power available to them. She stared down at the cover of her Bible, imprinted with her name, grateful that even a capsule prayer at crucial times, like now, could provide her with the wisdom and strength for the task ahead.

"Let's see what's going out over the wires." Coy's voice brought her back to the moment as he tuned in a popular station.

"It's eleven-thirty in Colorado Springs," the rich voice of an announcer droned above the van heater. "The temperature is a sunny fifty degrees, with a high of forty-eight in the mountains."

Automatically Casey's brown eyes lifted to the distant sprawl of Pikes Peak, the gold-splashed foot-hills reminding her that the aspens would soon reach a crescendo of color. A wistful sigh escaped her as she pondered a day off for a quick trip up Ute Pass to the high country to catch the brilliant gleam of the aspens before the first snowfall.

"Listen," Coy nudged her, turning up the volume.

"This late bulletin just in," the casual voice tensed. "A verdict of guilty has been handed down in the trial of James Winston Holcomb. Details later. . . ."

"That's the first one Simpson has lost in a long time." Coy wheeled around the corner, screeching to a halt near the crowd-jammed courthouse. "Ready?" He glanced at Casey.

"Ready," she acknowledged, shoving the heavy door open, then scrambling down, wondering why her instincts hadn't alerted her to wear slacks today.

"Where do you want to start?" Coy asked, the Porta-Pak camera hoisted to his shoulder. John, trailing behind, hugged cords and mikes.

Casey scanned the crowd, searching for those who looked willing to express an opinion.

"Look!" John's thin voice halted them. "There's Steve Simpson coming out a side door."

Casey's startled gaze flew to the distant figure. A dark, pin-striped suit neatly encased broad shoulders and long legs, now stretched forward in a hurried stride. The man was making his way down the back steps in an effort to escape the crowd, which was temporarily diverted near the front entrance. The dark head was lowered in brooding contemplation.

Casey recalled Simpson's other television appearances where he had entranced audiences with his rugged good looks, while the ice-blue gaze silenced irrelevant questions. He could be a real charmer, or he could slice to shreds any reporter who attempted to cast him in an unfavorable light.

Steve Simpson always appeared cool and poised. Never unprepared or inept. Losing this case must have been a real blow to his ego. To approach him now, Casey thought, would be like stepping into the cage with a grizzly bear. And yet. . .

"Let's get a statement!" she called over her shoulder, taking off across the courthouse grounds.

"The other crew probably already got one!" John yelled after her.

"Not if he took a back door!" she shouted, racing in pursuit of the retreating figure. "Mr. Simpson! Wait!"

The long legs stretched on, the man making no acknowledgment of her presence.

12

"Mr. Simpson!" Casey yelled again, gulping for breath.

He whirled, a threatening frown clouding his handsome face when he spotted the television camera on big Coy Wilkens's shoulder.

"Mr. Simpson, I'm Casey Green from Channel 6 News," she smiled brightly, struggling for composure.

He gave a brisk nod. "I made a statement earlier. I have nothing more to say."

The rich voice was loaded with scarcely suppressed anger, matching the slash of dark brows and the steel glint in his ocean-blue eyes. Casey swallowed, scrutinizing the hard-set jaw and jutting chin, marveling that a full mouth could be drawn in such a thin bitter line. Only the dark wavy hair offset the harsh planes of his face.

She felt a slight nudge between her shoulders and jerked her attention back to the task at hand.

"Mr. Simpson," she blinked at him, inching closer, aware that Coy was moving in behind her with the camera, "can't you give us just a few words . . ."

"No comment!" he snapped, turning away.

"*Wait!*"

The desperation in her voice spun him around again, the eyes blue stones now, chipping away at her self-confidence as he glared down at her diminutive frame as though she were a small yapping puppy obstructing his path.

"The public deserves to hear *your* side of the story," she further pressed. "You've maintained from the beginning that your client was innocent. Would you mind telling us just why you were so sure of this when eyewitnesses identified him as the thief?"

"I've already given my side of the story to a friend at the newspaper. You can read about it in the evening news."

Her mouth dropped open, his rudeness striking a raw nerve. If he could make a comment to the newspaper, why not to the television audience? This time her temper and her stubborn nature took over.

She threw an irritated glance at Coy who motioned her back toward Simpson, focusing the camera squarely on the tall man as the film began to roll.

Casey stalked after him, mentally berating him for his lack of cooperation, his arrogance, his conceit, and a dozen other things she was too frustrated to name.

There was only one sure way to gain his attention. She had to try it.

"Mr. Simpson!" Her voice was commanding; her tone, firm and authoritative. "How do you think losing this important case will affect your reputation as a winning attorney?"

The question directed upward to the rock-hard jaw had scarcely left her lips when he wheeled around with a cold fury that rocked her back on her heels.

"Obviously, I'm *not* a winning attorney," he growled. "I've just been informed that I'm a *lousy* attorney; that any decent lawyer would have won the case." The blue eyes darkened in wounded pride, the rich voice faltering. "Now you've got your statement," he said wearily, the very life drained from his words. "Are you satisfied?"

She stood speechless, stepping back from the cutting blue glare as he turned and walked away, the broad shoulders drooping.

"Hey, you were great!" Coy lowered the camera, staring after the disappearing attorney. "You captured his vulnerable side, and nobody's put that on film—ever!"

"Maybe," Casey sighed, lifting a hand to massage the tense muscles in her neck, "but I don't feel good

14

about it, Coy." She shook her head slowly, her gaze following the proud dark head and dejected figure.

"Ah, come on! It takes guts to be a good reporter." Coy gave her small shoulder a reassuring tap.

"Then maybe I just lost some of my ambition." She hugged her arms against herself, suddenly cold despite the warm sun.

"Coy, we still have film left, haven't we?" John interrupted tactfully.

"Yeah. Enough for another interview." Coy's gaze moved to the people still milling about the front entrance. "Come on, Green." Coy shifted the camera onto his broad shoulder. "Your work's not done yet."

"All right, let's go." Casey marshalled some enthusiasm. "Where do we start?"

"Let's check out the crowd—which was supposed to be the reason we came in the first place." Coy lumbered off, John close on his heels.

Casey squared her shoulders and set off across the grounds, willing her mind to function again. Her brown eyes scanned the faces, seeking a willing subject, yet another face haunted her still, the cold blue gaze piercing her conscience.

She bit her lip, guiltily recalling the manner in which she had pursued Simpson—circling him mentally, analyzing his weakness, then swooping in like a hunter stalking his prey. She had sensed a vulnerable spot and gone for it—ruthlessly, thoughtlessly, shamelessly. It was unlike her to be so callous and insensitive, but then he was the first person who had ever prodded her into losing her temper during an interview.

What was there about the man that set her on edge? That made her violate the basic Christian principle of compassion? Talking tough was not Casey's style, was not even consistent with her personal convictions. She operated, from a code of conduct based on

15

a biblical injunction recorded nearly two thousand years ago.

She shook her head, forcing the corners of her mouth into a tense smile that trembled momentarily, then faded.

She owed Steve Simpson an apology!

CHAPTER 2

"I THINK YOU'RE mean!" shouted an angry little voice as Casey gripped the telephone, wide-eyed, trying to ignore the racket in the newsroom and concentrate on the caller.

"I beg your pardon?" she managed finally. "Who's speaking?"

"My name's Brad and you're a mean reporter!" he repeated, more loudly this time. "You made my dad look bad on television last night and . . ."

"Your dad?" Casey frowned, thinking back to the previous evening.

"Steve Simpson is my dad," the tone softened momentarily, "and you made him feel awful! He's gone off skiing, and now I'm leaving too! *I hate you*!" The little voice cracked a second before the phone clicked in her ear.

Casey shook her blond head, her thoughts spinning. She lowered the phone to the cradle and sat dazedly trying to piece together the indignant message, shouted above the roar of a familiar noise she couldn't pinpoint.

Brad Simpson . . . Steve Simpson . . .

She propped an elbow on her desk, cupping her chin in her palm as she lifted her thoughtful gaze to the far window, her eyes seeking the snow-capped mountain range to the west.

She searched her mind for the information on the Simpson family, recalling how the death of Scarlett Simpson—Mrs. Steve Simpson—had taken precedence over all local news shortly after Casey had begun work at the station.

The lovely fashion model had earned wide acclaim, yet the public tribute to her was a token of respect to her husband, as well. For with the announcement of Scarlett's death had come the brief account of Steve Simpson's brilliant career. Survivors included a young son . . .

Casey sighed, recalling the little boy's tormented words. She hadn't realized when she prodded Simpson to make his vulnerable reply that she would be hurting a child, too.

"Ben—" Her eyes fell on the lanky man hurrying past her desk.

He whirled, brows arched questioningly.

"Ben, tell me about Steve Simpson," she asked quickly. "I just got a complaint from his son about my interview."

Ben shrugged, raking a hand through his touseled hair. "Simpson is shrewd, intelligent, and very private. Lost his wife a couple of years ago to some rare disease. Afterwards, he threw himself headlong into work and hasn't come up for air since."

He fidgeted, eager to be gone.

"I see," Casey murmured, her eyes narrowing as his words penetrated. "Thanks."

Absently she turned back to the telephone, her

18

clear-polished nails tapping a rhythm on the desk as her mind zipped back to her conversation with Brad.

Not only did she owe Steve an apology, she owed one to Brad.

"Get tough, Casey," Ben Steele had advised. "You'll never make it in this business if you take every interview so seriously."

But when Casey considered his advice, she decided the dimension of caring that she brought to her work was the very ingredient that set her apart, that made the public respond so easily to her. *Sometimes it's best to go with your instincts*, she thought.

She took a deep breath and reached for the telephone directory, her fingernail making a sweep down the yellow page under the column of attorneys. Locating Simpson's name, she dialed the office number, phrasing a conversation in her mind, certain all the while that Brad was bluffing about his father's leaving.

To her surprise an efficient-sounding secretary informed her that Mr. Simpson was out of town for the remainder of the week.

Thanking the secretary, she hung up, remembering Brad's last words . . . *Now I'm leaving too.*

What did he mean by that? she wondered, brows knitted. In the child's state of mind, leaving surely meant running away!

Quickly she dialed the home telephone number, tension building within her as she waited for an answer. Finally a woman's voice came on the wire, announcing the Simpson residence.

"May I speak with Brad, please?" Casey asked politely.

There was a slight hesitation. "He isn't here. Who's calling?"

Casey took only a second to ponder using a

fictitious name, then in her typical straightforward manner, she replied honestly to the question.

"Casey Green? What do you want *now*?" the voice demanded.

"I had a call from Brad earlier," she explained, overlooking the woman's sharp tone. "I merely wanted to apologize."

Silence filled the wire before the woman continued in a more civil tone. "He hasn't come home from school yet."

"Not yet?" Casey glanced at the wall clock. "Isn't he running a bit late?"

"Yes," the woman admitted grudgingly. "I was just going to send the gardener around the neighborhood to look for him. But what concern is it of yours?" she snapped, remembering.

Casey scooted to the edge of the chair, ignoring the small voice in her brain that warned her not to get involved. "May I come over, please? I think I should relate the phone conversation to you. I'm afraid there may be a problem. . . ."

"If you're just looking for another story," the woman cut her short, "don't bother."

"I assure you I'm *not* looking for another story," Casey replied emphatically. "You have my word that none of this will reach the media."

"All right," the woman conceded. "I *am* worried, quite frankly. And Mr. Simpson has gone to Vail for a few days' rest."

"Please give me your address," Casey grabbed a note pad and reached for a pen. "I'll come right over."

After jotting down the address, Casey ripped off the note and stuck it in the pocket of her gray flannel slacks. Saying a hurried good-by, she hung up the phone and grabbed her tote bag, making a dash for the back door. She paused as Mona, the secretary, shot her a questioning glance.

"Mona, I'll be out for a while," she called over her shoulder.

"Anything wrong?" The girl looked up from her desk, her mop of brown curls falling low over her forehead, shadowing green eyes behind gold-rimmed glasses.

"No," Casey forced a smile, "A personal matter."

"Want to leave a number where you can be reached?"

When Casey dismissed the suggestion with a wave of her hand, Mona nodded thoughtfully, misinterpreting her words. "Have fun, then."

Casey's lips parted to voice a denial, then clamped them firmly shut, preferring to let the girl think she was meeting someone for coffee.

Grabbing her navy blazer, she glanced over her shoulder to catch Mona's knowing grin. Perhaps Mona would quit nagging her to get herself a man if she believed she were up to something. She gave the secretary a broad smile, then flew out the door and down the steps to the parking lot, the big door banging shut behind her as she stepped out into the cold afternoon.

Her brown gaze lifted to sullen gray skies, the low moaning wind causing her to shiver into her light woolen blazer. A cold front had moved in during the morning, bringing a sharp sting to the mountain air and chasing the sun deeper into the clouds.

By the time Casey reached her small sports car, she was half-frozen. With a pang of concern, she thought of Brad. Had he worn a heavy coat when he left for school this morning? If he had left for school! Or had he merely pretended he was going to school, then taken off someplace right after breakfast? Surely he was all right, or he wouldn't be calling her!

21

Casey hopped into the cold leather seat and fished a silver ring of keys from her purse. Her slim fingers, stiff from the cold, fumbled for the car key. As she inserted the key in the ignition and cranked the engine, she found herself pondering the wisdom of a trip to the Simpson home. *Why am I doing this*? she wondered suddenly, a blank expression filling her brown eyes. *Why couldn't I have just repeated Brad's message to the housekeeper?* Besides, the child had probably merely gone to a friend's house after school rather than returning home. Quite likely, she was off on a wild goose chase.

Why am I doing this? Casey continued her self-interrogation as she maneuvered her little car expertly through the afternoon traffic along Pikes Peak Avenue.

"Because I feel partly responsible," she admitted. "I've never been so—" she bit her lips, slowing for a traffic light, "—so insensitive in my entire career as a reporter."

Other reporters pursued, tantalized, aggravated. Such tactics seemed to go with the territory. But she was *not* other reporters. She was Cassandra Louise Green, a Texas-born Christian who lived by the Golden Rule and who attributed her small degree of success to her determination to live by her Christian standards.

She glanced around her, aware that she had reached the exclusive Broadmoor area, situated on one of the foothills that commanded an impressive view of the city below.

She guided the wheel with her left hand, while she plunged into her right pants pocket, retrieving the crumpled note to verify the street and house number.

Ahead, three-story brick homes and low, ranch-style complexes stretched for half a block. She blinked, glancing past emerald lawns and towering rows of protective shrubs to the driveway marked 1507, then turned her car up the sweeping driveway to the quiet, Spanish home that was a pleasant departure from the stately brick dwellings. Despite the pleasant white exterior and red tiled roof, the desperate stillness of the place brought a shiver racing down her spine as she cut the engine and sat staring for a moment at the isolated house and grounds.

There were no shouts of playful children, no vibrations from stereos or televisions, not even the sound of bike tires on the smooth pavement behind her. The neighborhood was depressingly silent, and she found it hard to imagine a little boy flourishing here.

Casey sighed, reaching for her tote bag and hooking it over her shoulder as she hopped out of the car. She followed the stone walk that curved past carefully clipped shrubs and empty flower beds, past a manicured lawn that bore no evidence of children at play, up to the circular steps leading to the front door.

Squaring her shoulders, she lifted her hand to the brass knocker and let it fall. The heavy thud magnified in her ears, while the low moan of the wind echoed through the stillness.

Slowly the door opened, and she stood facing a gray-haired woman, fiftyish and plump, her round face lined with worry.

"Hello," Casey smiled. "I'm Casey Green."

"I know who you are." The woman gave a brisk nod and pushed the door open, her slow movements revealing her reluctance to admit Casey.

"And you're —" Casey extended her hand, determined to be friendly.

"Martha Browning, the housekeeper. I've been with the Simpsons for nearly ten years," she replied softly, her work-roughened hand gripping Casey's momentarily before retreating to her apron pocket.

23

"What did Brad say to you over the phone?" she leaned closer, her head inclined for the answer. "And why did he call *you*?"

Casey paused, studying the woman who was attempting to capture a tumbling gray strand from the smooth cap of hair drawn into a bun at her neck.

Martha was scarcely taller than Casey, yet she was many pounds heavier—the image of a motherly confidante. And the troubled look in her hazel eyes betrayed a vulnerability that made Casey want to throw her arms around her in mutual comfort rather than bear the bad news she had come to tell. She looked away from the imploring eyes, her gaze traveling over the stone foyer, and lingering on the closed doors of the formal Spanish interior.

"Could we sit down, please?" Casey asked, shoving her hands into her pants pockets in an effort to warm them.

"I'm sorry. Do come in." The woman led the way down a corridor to another closed door. Beyond this massive door, Casey saw a large room filled with overstuffed chairs and sofas, ornate mahogany tables, and towering brass lamps.

"We can talk here in the den," Martha motioned Casey in, flicking on lights to offset the musty gloom.

Casey's heels sank into the plush carpet as she crossed the room and seated herself in a chair, while Martha stood nervously twisting her hands.

"Brad called to scold me about the interview." Casey looked across at Martha's troubled face. "And then he said, 'My father has gone off skiing, and now I'm leaving, too!' "

"What did he mean by that?" Martha asked, her voice filled with frustration. "He didn't tell me he was going anywhere." She hugged her arms to her ample bosom, as though trying to warm herself against the stark cold truth. "I sent Herbert—that's our gardener—around the neighborhood to check on him. Nobody has seen him!"

"I think he meant he was running away from home," Casey said gently, saddened by the woman's pale drawn face.

"Oh, no!" Martha wailed. "After all we've been through—" she broke off, making a dash for the telephone on the desk. "I'll call his teacher to see if he was at school today." Her fingers trembled on the telephone dial.

Casey rose from her seat to pace the room, her troubled glance falling on the framed photograph of a young boy.

She crossed to the desk and lifted the picture, studying the small face before her. Perfectly chiseled features beneath a mop of dark hair stared up at her. Brad could have been the typical seven- or eight-year-old boy—and yet she felt sure that he was not. Despite the angular face, prominent ears, pert nose, and tilted smile, there was a seriousness beyond his years in the wide blue stare. The eyes, like the father's, were indeed a deep rich blue, but the poise and confidence of Steve Simpson seemed to be missing in his only child.

Casey replaced the photograph, her eyes lingering thoughtfully.

Brad looked—confused, she decided finally. Perhaps the air of assurance would come in later years, after he had solved the mysteries of his own little world.

"He didn't go to school today!" Martha cried, dropping the telephone awkwardly, before scrambling for it, then replacing it on the hook. "He *has* run away! You were right!" She sank into a chair, tears gathering in her frightened eyes.

Casey moistened her lips, struggling for words of consolation, yet knowing instinctively that Martha

25

had every reason to be distraught. "Children often run away from home just to prove something." She forced a light tone to her voice. "Sometimes they're back in time for dinner. Maybe that's what Brad will do," she suggested. Yet she heard the sound of fear in her own voice and realized even as she attempted to be optimistic, that other fears, worse fears, were forming in her own mind.

A vulnerable little boy running away from home was bad enough. When that boy also happened to be the son of a well-known attorney who could pay a hefty ransom. . .

Casey shoved her hands deep into her pockets again, the flannel lining failing to warm them. She stared down at the carpet, her thoughts racing.

"I've had a sick feeling in the pit of my stomach all week," Martha's voice trembled. "Mr. Simpson's been so involved with this trial that he's hardly had time to speak to the rest of us. Brad's birthday was last Wednesday. He just turned eight. Mr. Simpson missed our birthday supper—" she broke off, wiping the tears from her cheeks with the corner of her apron. "Brad has seemed so lonely lately. We've got to call Mr. Simpson!" She jumped up from the chair and moved toward the telephone.

"He's at Vail, you said?" Casey asked tentatively.

Martha nodded. "He has a condominium up there. Of course, he'll be out on a ski slope now—" her words trailed away as she reached into the desk drawer, removing a small metallic directory.

"You know," Martha's eyes returned to Casey, "Brad begged to go with him. But Mr. Simpson was so worn out after the trial. Said he needed a few days to himself. Brad didn't understand," she sighed, turning back to the phone.

"I'll be going on the air soon," Casey said, glancing at her watch. "I must go. If you or Mr. Simpson need

26

to reach me, I'll be at the station until seven. After that, I'll be at my apartment. I'm listed in the directory," she added quickly.

"I just hope Brad's okay." Martha lifted bleak eyes to Casey. "I can't imagine where he'd run off to. He hasn't many friends."

Casey tried to imagine how Brad must feel. He had lost his mother to an early death, his father was overworked, and probably tense and irritable many evenings when he came home. And with few friends to confide in—Casey shook her head, aware that all the conditions were right for producing a problem child, or, as she preferred to believe, a child with problems.

"Try not to worry, Martha," Casey paused beside her, placing a reassuring hand on the plump arm. "We'll just have to pray that Brad will be fine."

"I haven't prayed in a long time," Martha's voice trembled as she lifted the receiver, "but I guess we'll all be learning how again—"

"Good idea," Casey replied. She managed a reassuring smile and walked quickly back up the hall. Lifting her jacket from the coat tree, she let herself out the front door, then hesitated on the front steps, her brown eyes scanning the neighborhood.

There was something terribly depressing about the Simpson home, and her steps automatically quickened as she hurried back to her car.

Casey sat on the edge of a chair in the darkened editing room, going over last week's interview with a local politician. The interview had been one of her typical on-the-street clips, but this one had been unique in that she had captured the man and his son on their way into a fast-food establishment.

They had spent a few seconds discussing the merits

27

of hamburgers and french fries for growing boys before the politician adeptly maneuvered the subject to his upcoming election.

"He's a cool one," the film editor commented as he checked the frames, "but he lacks something."

"Charisma, Sam," Casey nodded. "I noticed that, too."

"Too bad Simpson doesn't run for office," Sam offered idly, unaware that the name had brought Casey upright. "That guy's middle name is charisma! All he has to do is walk into a room and open his mouth, and everybody stops to listen."

"How do you know?" Casey turned to him curiously, oblivious to the footage running unnoticed on the screen.

"I sat in on one of his trials. Man, that guy could sell refrigerators to Eskimos. He's something!"

Casey swallowed, turning back to the smiling politician still rambling on. She stared at the blond man on the screen, visualizing in his place the dark commanding presence of Steve Simpson.

Sam's probably right, she thought, remembering how she had stood mesmerized on the courthouse steps before she could propel herself into action.

She stood up, suddenly nervous and jumpy. "I think that looks okay, don't you, Sam? If Ben agrees, we'll use it one night this week."

"Yeah, it's okay." Sam flicked the lights on, grinning across at her. "You're the one who should run for office, you know. You have a way with people."

Casey waved a hand of dismissal at his teasing grin, ignoring his inference that her successful interviews were a result of manipulating her subjects through her good looks or charm. She prided herself on her ability to create rapport with the person on the street, but it

28

would have been a compromise of her convictions to use feminine wiles rather than intelligence and skill.

She hurried back down the corridor to the newsroom, Ben's deep voice halting her as she rounded a corner.

"Hey, Casey! I took a look at the footage on that Jenkins guy this afternoon. Good job." He caught up with her, giving her a nod of approval as they walked back to the newsroom.

"Mr. Jenkins was a delightful interview," she smiled up at Ben. "Can you imagine yourself walking four miles a day when you're eighty-three? He never misses a morning, he told me."

Ben groaned. "I can't pull *one* mile at forty-two." His lanky stride slackened at the thought.

"You easily cover a dozen miles a day just pacing around this building," Casey laughed as they turned into the wide door of the newsroon.

"Casey! Hey, Casey! Hurry up! You're wanted on the phone," someone yelled. "It's some kid."

Casey's mind began to work as she raced across to her desk, scrambling for the phone.

"Didn't know you were so fond of kids," a reporter grinned, sauntering past her desk.

She shot him a warning glance, still trying to think of what she would say to Brad. She took a deep breath, forcing a calmness to her tone as she answered.

For a moment there was no reply to her hello, just light breathing.

"Hello! Who's there?" She gripped the phone tighter.

"You didn't tell them I'd run away."

Casey blinked, for a moment too confused by his words to grasp their meaning. "Tell who?" she frowned. "Your father and Martha?"

He huffed an impatient sigh. In that quiet second, a

public address system announced a twenty-five percent discount on washers and dryers.

Casey gripped the receiver tighter, listening, aware that he was in a large store. *But where*?

"You didn't announce it on television!" he shouted.

Casey concentrated on his words, her mind probing for the proper replies. "Did you want me to?" she asked softly.

There was a slight hesitation again, a vibrating hum filling up the silence as Casey closed her eyes, struggling to remember where she had heard those sounds before.

"Well, I *have* run away!" his voice rose in an indignant protest. "Not that anybody cares!"

"Brad, listen to me," she took a deep breath, praying for the right words. "Lots of kids run away from home every day. And do you know what they discover?" she asked.

Another impatient sigh.

"They find out that what they run *to* is usually worse than what they ran *from*," she continued, not waiting for his reply. "You're not being fair, you know. I think you're blaming your father for something *I* did. I'm really sorry about that interview. I know that's what made you angry. Your dad is a wonderful attorney, and I should never have pressed him. Honey, he and Martha are worried sick over you!"

"They don't care!" he shouted. "Martha's always talking to her daughter over the phone. And all Dad thinks about is his old clients. He cares more about them than he does about me!"

"Brad, that's not true!" Casey gasped, realizing suddenly she had no idea about the boy's true relationship with his father. In any case she found it hard to believe that Steve Simpson did not love his

30

son. "If you'll just come back home, you'll see you're wrong and—"

"No! I'm never coming back," he threatened, his voice trembling.

In the following second of complete silence, she strained her ears to pick up the voice in the background. This time the sound was distinct and clear.

"Stop by the tire center for Sears two-for-one sale!"

She recognized the voice coming from a speaker and suddenly the words were intelligible.

"Brad!" Casey bolted upright in her chair, her mind racing. "If I can get a special news bulletin about you flashed on during the next half-hour of programming, could you watch it? Is there a television set nearby?"

"Yeah! I can see several televisions where I am," he boasted.

"Great!" She was already getting to her feet, reaching for her tote bag. "You stay right where you are and watch those TV screens. I'll try to get that bulletin on within the next half-hour. Okay?"

"Okay! But make it good," he added, a note of triumph in his little voice.

"I will! Stay near those television sets," she urged before saying good-by.

As soon as the line clicked, she hung up to break the connection, then quickly lifted the phone again, her fingers zipping over the numbers as she dialed the Simpson home. A rich male voice answered on the first ring and she realized, heart pounding, that Steve Simpson had returned.

"Mr. Simpson?" she asked tentatively.

"Yes? Who is it?" he barked impatiently.

"This is Casey Green! I think I've located Brad." The words burst from her throat.

"What? How? The police have looked everywhere!"

31

"He called me again, this time wanting to know why I hadn't broadcast his runaway over the news. Earlier I had detected voices and noises I couldn't identify. This time I distinctly heard a public address system announcing the tire sale at *Sears*. I'm positive that's where he is."

"I thought the police checked all the stores." His voice softened.

"When I asked if Brad was where he could watch a television if I put on the news bulletin he wanted, he said he could watch *several*. I'm going there now," she added, unwilling to waste more time in lengthy explanations. "Good-by."

"I'll meet you there!" he yelled in her ear as she replaced the phone and darted out of the newsroom.

Casey drove recklessly through the freezing night, making the parking lot at Sears in record time.

She tried to pace her steps as she headed through the front door, then halted beside the appliances, peering carefully around a refrigerator to the entertainment center where several television sets were going full blast. She saw him immediately—a small, dark-haired boy, his gaze fastened on the largest screen.

She took a step forward, then hesitated. What would she say to him? And would he bolt when he realized she had tricked him?

She retreated to her vantage point, watching him closely.

"Could I help you?" asked a voice from behind her.

She jumped, whirling to face an equally surprised salesman.

"Hey, you're the girl who does the on-the-street interviews, aren't you?" The young man's eyes widened with interest. "Are you looking for a refrigerator? Or someone to interview?'' he added with a grin.

She tried to control her frantic breathing, aware for the first time how fast her heart was beating.

''I'm meeting someone,'' she smiled at him. ''May I wait here?''

''Any old time,'' he quipped. ''May I show you our new line of refrigerators while you're waiting?''

She glanced over her shoulder to be sure Brad was still positioned on a footstool near the television. ''Not now, thanks. Maybe another time,'' she offered, not wanting to offend him or call attention to herself.

As she glanced back toward Brad, she noticed a policeman strolling by. He cast an appraising look at Brad, then walked on. A few steps beyond, the officer paused beside a stove to peer inside the oven while surreptitiously giving Brad another glance.

Casey took a deep breath, realizing the police had been alerted, and that Steve was either on his way or was already on the premises. Brad was fidgeting now, turning slowly to gaze inquisitively at the policeman. Casey ducked behind a refrigerator, pretending a sudden interest in the icemaker.

''Did you change your mind?'' The eager salesman rushed up.

She took a deep breath, struggling for patience. ''No, I was just curious.''

When she slipped back to check on Brad, she saw that Steve had arrived, and that the two were embracing, oblivious to the stares of curious onlookers.

Casey bit her lip, hesitating to intrude on their reunion. When Steve's moist blue eyes lifted above the boy's head, widening suddenly at the sight of her, she merely lifted her hand in a reassuring wave, then turned and walked quickly out of the store.

33

She couldn't bring herself to face Brad, knowing she had betrayed him. But at least he was back with his father, and that was the important thing.

Maybe both of them had learned a lesson.

Remembering her hasty exit, Casey decided to check in at the office before going home for the night. Ben, who seemed to sleep and eat in his glass-enclosed office, was working late. As she passed his door, he gave her a silent salute, still cradling the telephone against his shoulder.

Waving back, Casey hurried on, hoping she had misinterpreted the look of quiet panic on his face. Clearing her desk, then locking the drawers, she was preparing to leave when she caught a glimpse of Ben's long legs swiftly closing the distance between them.

"Aren't you overdoing your dedication to WJAK?" she asked teasingly.

"Hal's sick and the lumber company on Colorado Avenue is on fire!" He waved a scribbled note. "Crew Three is covering. Get over there. We'll hold a slot on the wrap-up tonight."

"But—" her brown eyes widened in protest as she stared up into his stern face, her lips forming a desperate plea that died in her throat as she glanced around the deserted newsroom.

"You're a slave driver, Ben Steele!" She yanked the paper from his hand, whirling back for her tote bag. "You know I don't like fires. And Coy might have a lead foot, but he's no firetruck chaser!"

Her lips thinned in frustration as she groped for a sharpened pencil, then dropped it into her bulging bag. A nagging voice within reminded her that it had taken two years to earn the distinction of being one of the station's best reporters. If she wanted to protest overwork, she must do it later in a more businesslike manner. A point of discussion tomorrow, she vowed, glancing over her shoulder at Ben, already absorbed in another telephone conversation.

She trudged out the door, her small chin thrust forward in defiance. *Tomorrow*, she vowed. But for now there was a building on fire. . . .

Exhaustion crept into every bone in Casey's body as she dragged herself up the steps to her apartment, aware that the hour was late. Her body screamed for a bath, followed by twelve hours of uninterrupted sleep. The phone was ringing as she unlocked the door, hurriedly flipping on a light in the hall, then tripping over a discarded houseshoe in her cluttered path to the persistent phone.

"Hello!" she shouted irritably, cradling the phone against her shoulder as she leaned over to drag her leather boots from sore aching feet. Frowning at the blister on her big toe, she was caught momentarily off guard when a masculine voice filled the wire.

"Miss Green? This is Steve Simpson." His voice held a note of apology.

"How's Brad?" she asked quickly, sinking onto the sofa.

"He's fine. I didn't get a chance to thank you tonight," he said softly.

"I'm just glad I could help," she replied, her brown gaze focused on the circle of light on her carpet. His tone was so different from her mental image of the man that she found herself at a loss for words. "Would it be possible for me to speak to Brad?" she asked suddenly. "I feel I owe him an apology. I did make him a promise."

"He's already in bed," Steve hesitated, "and it might be better to wait. He's a little upset with you right now. With everyone. Please understand."

"I do understand." She closed her eyes, thinking of the vulnerable little voice that had begged for attention. "Where was he all day? Did you find out?"

"He just wandered around the shopping center, somehow managing to elude everyone who was looking for him. When Martha called, I chartered a plane home immediately. We were frantic," he added, the tension mounting in his voice.

"Well, I'm so glad he's home safely, Mr. Simpson."

"Steve," he interrupted. "Since you've been involved in our family trauma, we should at least be on a first-name basis."

"About the interview," she continued. "I really don't know what came over me. I've never been such a pest—"

"You were merely doing your job," he interrupted. "I respect that, even if I didn't approve of your doing that job on *me*," he added, chuckling softly.

The sound of his laughter was more surprising than another tongue-lashing. She swallowed, struggling against the strange sensation filtering through her on hearing his pleasant voice.

"Well, I think I overdid it. I had no right to provoke you that way."

"Let's just forget the entire incident. I was overwrought from the trial, and more than a little angry with my client who had just bawled me out for losing the case. I did the best I could, but now I just want to put the whole matter behind me."

Casey laughed softly. "I'll be more than happy to forget that incident," she agreed.

"Now back to my reason for calling. I wanted to invite you to dinner at our house tomorrow evening. Would you join us—Brad and me? The poor little guy is pretty embarrassed about everything, but I suppose that's normal."

36

"I suppose," Casey bit her lip, wondering if anything Brad had done could be considered normal.

Dinner? With Steve Simpson? And his unpredictable son?

She frowned.

The rich voice filled her ears again, this time more persuasively. "I feel we owe you something. Please allow us to make amends. Even Martha insists."

"All right," Casey decided, strangely unable to say no. "But my work schedule won't allow me to be definite about the hour, I'm afraid."

"Just come when you're free," he suggested, his voice lifting pleasantly. "Martha can prepare a meal that will keep in the oven. I'm taking the day off. I intend to spend more time with Brad. I've learned something from all this, I hope."

His relief at having his son back was evident.

"Perhaps we all have," she replied. "Enjoy your day with Brad, and I'll see you tomorrow evening. Good night, Steve." She placed the phone on the cradle and stretched out on the sofa.

Casey lay still, savoring the peaceful moment and thinking about the Scripture verse which promises that all things work together for good to those who love God. Perhaps the temporary anguish suffered during Brad's disappearance had been worth the cost.

Her brown eyes drifted toward the ceiling, a smile lighting her weary features.

"Thank You," she whispered.

CHAPTER 3

"EVERYONE READY?" Casey asked the group of wide-eyed children. "Don't be afraid of the camera or the microphone. All you have to do is tell me what you like most about the circus. Think you can handle that?" she asked with a smile.

She was greeted by a chorus of enthusiastic responses as the boys and girls nudged each other, then stood waiting.

"Ready, Coy?" she glanced over her shoulder.

Coy frowned in reply. In John's absence, he was finding that handling both camera and sound equipment was no easy task, with children stumbling over wires and a crowd gathering at the sight of a television camera. Focusing the lens, he nodded to Casey, then started the film rolling.

"Come to the circus! Join the razzle-dazzle in the big arena where a sell-out crowd is gathering! The circus came to Colorado Springs today and the entire town seems to have captured the excitement. Why do people come to the circus?" her voice rose questioningly, her blond head inclined in a gesture of curiosity. "We decided to ask the real experts."

She leaned down, extending the microphone to a small black boy whose dark eyes had widened to enormous proportions. "I came to see Dumbo the elephant," he said.

"I came to see the clowns," a little girl giggled as Casey moved the microphone along the group.

"I like to see the pretty ladies up on the high wire," one red-headed boy confessed, a mischievous smile dimpling his face.

Casey laughed, aware that his comment had brought this segment to a satisfactory conclusion. She straightened to her full height, smiling into the camera.

"Whatever the reason, there's nothing quite like a circus to make all of us feel young at heart," she paused, her brown eyes thoughtful. "This is Casey Green, Channel 6 News."

"A take!" Coy nodded, lowering the heavy camera.

"Thanks, kids." Casey unhooked the microphone and waved to the group. "You can see yourselves on the news tonight at six o'clock. Have fun!"

Her little audience whooped their response, then dashed off to join the line forming at the front entrance to the auditorium.

"Whew, what a day!" She glanced at Coy as they climbed back into the van.

Casey leaned back in the seat, closing her eyes in an effort to relax as Coy cranked the engine and spun away from the curb. She had spent a hectic morning, rushing from one location to another, with Ben thrusting an assignment in her face each time she slowed down to catch her breath. While she had performed her tasks with the usual diligence, one part of her consciousness centered on Brad and Steve, each presenting a different problem.

She prayed that Brad had forgiven her and that this dinner together would somehow make things right between them. Reaching for her tote bag, Casey remembered the two free circus tickets she had been given as a member of the press. Maybe Brad would want to go. Regaining his trust would not be easy, but perhaps this would be a start.

She thought of Steve again, wondering why he lingered in her mind. She had lain awake last night, despite utter exhaustion, pondering Steve's strange effect on her, mentally debating with herself that this nervousness was merely connected to her concern for Brad. But that was just an excuse, she had finally conceded, knowing all too well that the man set her on edge like a flash of lightning streaking through a summer sky.

Coy swung into the parking lot and was cutting the engine as she roused up in her seat, a weary yawn escaping her.

"I've had a craving for Mexican food all day," Coy stroked his heavy beard. "Want to try that new place over in Uintah?" he asked, reaching into the back seat for his camera.

Casey shook her head. "The only Mexican food that interests me is served back in Fort Worth by real Mexicans who know what they're doing."

"You Texans!" Coy snorted. "Think you do everything bigger and better. Well, what's next?" he nodded toward the clipboard lying in the front seat.

"This is it, I hope," she moaned, pressing a hand to her weary forehead. "Can you rush that film over to Editing so they can see how it looks? In the meantime I'll check my desk for messages. Thanks, Coy, and I'll take a raincheck on that Mexican dinner."

She gathered up the clipboard, along with her tote bag, and climbed down from the van. Hurrying across the parking lot to the back door, she prayed this would be her last assignment for the day.

Deep in thought, she stepped through the slow-moving doors of the elevator and absently punched the button, watching the lights flick on the floor numbers as the elevator swung into gear. She glanced down at her still-fresh sweater and slacks, deciding that it would not be necessary to change before going to the Simpsons' for dinner.

Stepping off the elevator, Casey headed for Ben's office, ready now for that confrontation about her overloaded schedule. Nothing was going to prevent her from keeping her date this evening, she decided, her chin thrust forward in defiance.

Later, as Casey arrived at the Simpson house, her neat appearance belied her hectic day. Her efforts to convince Ben that she was overworked had been waved aside with a rash of compliments and a cunning grin. Still, her work load *had* lightened, and now she was arriving before dark, like any other respectable dinner guest.

Hurrying up the walk to the front door, the wind whistled down the pine-studded foothills, nipping at her face and whipping her hair into tangled gold. The cold front had moved out, leaving only brisk air in its wake, but the slightly piercing sting was invigorating. Casey found herself looking forward to the evening ahead.

The front door swung open at her knock, and Martha stood smiling, her hazel eyes reflecting a look of relief.

"Come in, Miss Green! Here, let me take your coat. It feels wintry out there tonight."

"Yes, it does," Casey nodded, appreciating the cozy warmth of the house as she slipped out of her heavy camelhair coat and rubbed her hands together to warm her numb fingers.

"Mr. Simpson and Brad are in the den," Martha indicated with a nod, then turned to hang Casey's coat on the hall tree. When she looked at Casey, there was an inscrutable expression on her face. Despite her polite manner, Casey sensed some kind of inner conflict.

"Fine, I'll join them there." Casey smoothed the wrinkles from her red sweater and navy slacks as she hurried down the hall.

She paused in the doorway, her gaze skimming the two dark heads bent over a chessboard as father and son sat in contemplative silence. She had a sudden impulse to turn around and tiptoe away, not wanting to intrude on this special moment.

But then Steve's dark head spun around perceptively, the blue gaze widening in acknowledgment of her presence.

"Come in, Casey," he stood, motioning her to join them.

Brad's head jerked up, the sight of Casey coloring his thin cheeks crimson. He leapt to his feet to make a dash from the room, but Steve's long arm shot out to capture him. He held the boy firmly in a gentle grip.

"Wait, Brad," he commanded in a tone of quiet authority.

"Hello there," Casey smiled, her pleasant expression failing to betray the sharp sting she felt at his rejection. She lifted her leather clutch purse and snapped it open. "I have two front-row seats at the circus." She waved the tickets proudly.

"I don't like the circus," he glared at her.

"What do you mean you don't like the circus? Why, I'll bet you've never even ridden an elephant!"

Her gaze slipped back to Steve who stood observing the parley between them in quiet amusement.

42

"Why would I want to ride an elephant?" the child's tone softened, curiosity and excitement overriding his anger.

"Well, I guess you'd just have to ride one to find out," Casey shrugged lightly. "But I'll bet you a giant bag of popcorn that you'd have such a good time you'd probably want to join the circus and become an animal trainer!"

"Sounds great to me," Steve beamed at her, his approval obvious. "Okay with you, Brad?"

The old tension returned as Brad stood glaring at the floor in sullen silence. When Martha appeared in the door to announce dinner, Casey smothered a sigh of frustration.

"Yes, I think we're all ready for one of your good dinners, Martha." Steve's broad shoulders drooped slightly as he cast a doubtful glance at Brad. "How about you, Casey?"

"Definitely," she nodded, trying to recall what she'd had for lunch and deciding she must have forgotten to eat.

"Then what are we waiting for?" Steve forced a stiff grin, his hand cupping Brad's shoulder, guiding him toward the dining room. Casey followed, wondering what in the world to say next.

The formality of the dining room seemed to add to the starched atmosphere. Steve seated her at the opposite end of the long table, with Brad to her right.

Casey tried to force an appreciative smile at the sight of the snowy linen tablecloth, the gleaming silver, the elegant china. The corners of her mouth refused to budge, however, aware of her stubborn belief that a cozy supper in the kitchen would have been easier for her first face-to-face encounter with Brad. She was still a stranger in this delicate situation, she reminded herself. She must try to keep a cool head until she felt more comfortable.

Leaning back against the ornate mahogany chair, she stole a glance at Brad, slumped over his plate. He seemed smaller and more vulnerable than his strong voice had indicated. Thick dark hair framed a thin face, the features a sharper version of his father's. The blue eyes were the same intense blue, but when Brad raised his gaze to her, a smouldering rebellion seemed to leap from their depths before the dark lashes drooped, shuttering his expression from her once more.

"My, this smells good, Martha," Casey commented to the white-aproned woman bearing a platter of roast beef, surrounded by baby carrots and potatoes.

"I hope you like it," Martha replied, glancing at Casey with that same peculiar expression before she placed the platter in the center of the table. Then she turned and hurried back to the kitchen.

Steve took a sip of water, his eyes meeting hers over the rim of the crystal goblet. Shaken by a jolting awareness of his masculinity, Casey busied herself with the crisp linen napkin, placing it carefully in her lap.

"Well, tell us about yourself," Steve began conversationally. "How did you happen to get into television reporting?"

"Almost by accident," she laughed. "I started out as a part-time reporter for a Texas paper. I worked during the summers while I was attending the University of Texas. After college I came here and got a job for WJAK as a gofer. You know, go for' this, go for' that?" She paused, the brown eyes sparkling with humor as she looked from Steve to Brad. "Because I like people and enjoy talking with them, I began to get a few small assignments, simple interviews, really, and just worked my way up."

Martha was placing vegetables and a basket of rolls before them, temporarily diverting their attention.

44

The yeasty aroma drifting up from the bread was tantalizing, and Casey tried to recall how long it had been since she had enjoyed a good home-cooked meal. It occurred to her that her drive for success had re-routed her from some of life's simplest, yet most enjoyable pleasures.

As Martha brought in the last platter, Casey sat waiting for someone to say grace before realizing that apparently she was the only one who had considered the idea.

"We watched you on the evening news," Steve picked up the conversation again. "That was a terrible fire over at the lumber company. Aren't you nervous about covering such dangerous assignments?"

She studied the silver meat fork as she lifted a slice of roast beef onto her plate, then added vegetables. "Fires definitely are not my favorite news story," she acknowledged with a grin. "But one of our top reporters is on vacation, leaving the rest of us to take up the slack."

"I think you're being modest." Steve watched as Martha filled his coffee cup from a silver pot. "I've noticed you're covering some pretty important people and events."

"Like the circus!" she laughed. "Actually, my specialty is on-the-street interviews. I like talking with the average person, trying to find something fresh and exciting in everyday life. I don't have any strong desire to get into hard news."

"That's very commendable," Steve nodded, sipping his coffee. "My experience with reporters has often been unpleasant, due to their efforts to make a flashy report rather than an accurate one."

While his remark had been innocently stated, the tense silence that followed hung thickly over the table, as the three of them recalled her brief interview with Steve only days ago.

Casey pushed the food around on her plate, trying to ignore the impact of his words, but Brad's piercing gaze left her no choice. Placing her fork on her plate, she leaned forward, meeting Brad's rebellious blue eyes with as much warmth as possible.

"I'm an honest person," Casey said evenly, "and when something is bothering me, I can't pretend. Brad, I know you're angry with me—first, because of the interview. I've already apologized for that. Now you're angry because you think I tricked you. You'll just have to believe me when I tell you that I had to! Your safety—maybe even your life—could have been in danger.

"The reason we at the station hesitate to broadcast the, er, disappearance of someone from a prominent family is that there are some people in the world who might try to use that kind of information for their own selfish reasons—for money, maybe. You could have been hurt—" she broke off, the sullen little face giving no indication that he was relating to what she was saying.

"I really would like for us to be friends, Brad." Casey extended her hand, her fingers outstretched to him. Trying a different approach, she invited, "Will you go to the circus with me?"

He leapt up, his chair bumping the table and sloshing the water from the crystal goblets. "I'll think about it," he mumbled, the words scarcely coherent as he bounded from the room.

"*Brad!*" Steve shouted, his face paling with anger.

"No, Steve, *please*," Casey pleaded, her brown eyes imploring. "Let him go. I don't want to push. He's right," she sighed, aware for the first time of how deeply Brad must have suffered in his short life.

"Something wrong with my dinner?" Martha marched in, hands on her hips, her hazel eyes wounded.

"The meal is wonderful, Martha." Steve stood up, folding his napkin beside his plate. "Brad's behavior just altered our appetite, that's all. Would you mind leaving the food in the oven? Perhaps later."

"Maybe you'd like to have coffee in your study, Mr. Simpson. You could talk privately there."

"Would you like that?" He looked down the long table to search Casey's eyes.

"Of course," she nodded, following him out of the room that only amplified the tension surrounding them. In the hallway Casey glanced across at Steve, noticing that he moved as though his ankles were weighted with lead. The broad shoulders had begun to slump.

He opened the door, then stood aside for her to enter.

Casey's gaze flew over the book-lined room, reflecting the personality of an intelligent, well-read man. She moved to the fireplace, warming herself before the embers of a dying fire.

"I'll stoke up that fire," Steve offered, reaching forward to open the screen and prod the logs with a brass poker.

Watching as he poked at the fire, she noted the broad set of his shoulders, the trim waist, the long legs that appeared even longer in slim navy pants. She turned away, wandering over to sink onto the over-stuffed sofa, warning herself that she must not become involved with this man and his son. She was merely a dinner guest in their home—nothing more.

Yet, in her heart, Casey knew that she was already very much involved. Strange, but she seemed to be forming some kind of link between Brad and his father. And despite her efforts to appear nonchalant about Steve Simpson, she could not remain indifferent each time his penetrating blue gaze held hers. Above all, her heart cried out for Brad, struggling beneath a heavy load of confusion and bitterness.

The newly tended fire leapt brightly before them, tossing dancing shadows over the paneled wall. Steve walked over to his recliner, wearily settling his long frame into the comfort of the brown tweed chair.

"I'm sorry," he turned to her, full lips drawn in a tight line.

She shifted, propping her elbow against a soft pillow. "Please don't apologize. I can understand how difficult it must be trying to raise a young boy alone—" she broke off, shocked by the sudden arch of his dark brows.

"We've managed," he replied coolly. "There haven't been any serious problems—until this trial." His words were heavily underscored, reminding Casey of her own dismal role in publicizing his most recent failure.

She blinked in confusion, wondering if she should be sympathetic or irritated. Wishing to be understood, she tried again, her brown eyes sincere.

"I just meant I appreciate the problems both of you must have had adjusting to the loss of your wife—"

Casey could have bitten off her tongue as she watched the darkly handsome face harden to a mask of bitterness. How could she have become so personal in these past minutes, she wondered frantically, when all she wanted was to express concern? She had assumed enough time had elapsed since Scarlett Simpson's death to allow a gentle reference to her, but Steve's tormented reaction shouted the truth into the sudden tense silence.

She got to her feet, hurt and humiliated by the turn of their conversation. Now she wanted only to escape this brooding man who had resisted all overtures of friendship and who was threatening to turn her own well-ordered world into utter chaos.

48

"Forgive me, Steve, I really must be going. I do hope you and Brad get everything straightened out between you."

"We'll get everything straightened out." Steve rose from the recliner. "But I'm afraid you're leaving with the impression that our situation is worse than it really is. What's the old saying?" he asked, the hard corners of his mouth turning upward in a sardonic smile. "'Call me anything, but don't call me a bad parent'!"

"I'm not calling you a bad parent." Her brows shot upward, amazed that he could so distort her meaning. "But I do think—" she paused, her conviction not to interfere fading with the realization that Steve was trying to ignore the problem.

"What do you think?" he asked, an edge to his tone.

"I think Brad needs some counseling. I know a wonderful Christian counselor—"

"Just a minute! Are you saying Brad needs to see a psychiatrist?" The blue eyes had turned stormy and the hard jaw and chin jutted stubbornly.

"Lots of children see counselors nowadays. Sometimes an outsider who is trained to deal with family problems can accomplish more than a parent who may have become overprotective or—"

"Overworked," he cut in angrily. "I know that's on the tip of your tongue, so I'll say it for you. Yes, I'm overworked. And, yes, I should have taken him with me to Vail. I'll spare you that observation. But I needed the time to myself."

"I wasn't about to say anything like that," she cried. "Will you please stop twisting my words?"

He glared at her, obviously expecting his cold silence to force her into a sudden apology or a hasty retreat from the room.

She stood her ground, determined not to be outdone, since she felt Brad's welfare was at stake.

Suddenly she was prepared to do battle for him—even if her opponent happened to be his father.

"And how many children do *you* have, *Miss Green*?" he growled, his sharp words slicing the chilly atmosphere.

She gasped at his cruelty. "I don't have *any* children. But if and when I do, I plan to make them feel loved and secure. I won't overprotect them and I won't overload myself with work. And if necessary, I wouldn't hesitate to seek professional help. I certainly wouldn't *run* from the problem, or pretend that it doesn't exist!"

The sudden silence that filled the room was charged with the electrical tension of strong emotions held in check. They stood glaring at each other, momentarily at a verbal impasse.

"Good night," she forced the words through trembling lips, as she turned to go.

He moved behind her in a polite pretense of seeing her to the door.

"I can find my way out!" she retorted, her dark eyes shooting sparks. "Don't bother!"

Head erect, she walked calmly through the door, then made a dash for the coat rack in the hall. Thrusting her arms through the sleeves of her coat, she opened the door and fled down the front steps, welcoming the blast of cold air that stung her face and made her blood race even faster.

"Good night and goodby!" she ground through clenched teeth as she raced back to the car.

The desk phone shattered Casey's quiet concentration as she studied the script for her next interview.

"Not again!" she moaned, wondering as she lifted the phone how many times she had been interrupted in the past hour.

"I decided I want to go to the circus, after all," came a small voice.

Casey had almost forgotten the rumpled circus tickets in her purse. She blinked, prodding her work-numbed brain a couple of turns before she could translate the words and the unspoken plea behind them.

"Brad, is that you?" she frowned, staring at the mountain of work overflowing her desk.

"Yes'm. Can we go? Please?"

Casey bit the inside of her lip, recalling his father's rude retort. She had made up her mind to stay away from the Simpsons and yet she couldn't bring herself to refuse Brad, although she wasn't certain why.

"Well, if you want to go—sure, we'll go! Shall I pick you up around seven? That is, if your father doesn't object," she added, her tone sharpening.

"Martha already said I could go. Besides, Dad's working late."

So the workaholic had already escaped by burying himself in the source of their problems! *Some people never learn*, she thought bitterly.

"I'll be ready whenever you say," Brad sounded excited, his happy voice drawing her back to the conversation.

"All right," she suppressed a sigh, "I'll come by for you at seven. And Brad, I'm glad you decided to go."

After she hung up, she sat staring at the phone. Perhaps it wasn't Brad who needed the counselor—perhaps it was his father!

On the way home from the circus, Brad chattered happily about the wonders he had seen for the first time that night—fourteen cages of tigers, prowling on velvet paws; great white stallions, muscles of steel

51

rippling beneath satin coats; high-wire artists perform-
ing their death-defying stunts on invisible wire suspended in space.

Casey couldn't resist a warm smile of affection as
she glanced down at the small boy, dressed in a long-
sleeved Panama Jack T-shirt and fashionably faded
Levis. His dark hair tumbled negligently around his
face; his blue eyes reflected fascination and delight.
She suppressed the urge to reach over and smooth
down the rebellious strands of hair. Their friendship
must evolve naturally—because he wanted it, too,
not because her heart was filling with love for him and
a strong maternal instinct that she was only now
beginning to recognize.

"Brad, I've been wondering," she ventured.
"Where do you go to Sunday school?" She was fairly
certain what his answer would be.

He glanced curiously at her then turned back to
inspect the sleek sports car ahead. "I don't go
anywhere."

"You don't?" she asked, his words confirming her
suspicions.

"Nope. Dad doesn't go to church, either. I've been
twice—both times when I visited my grandmother in
Illinois. We had to sit in a circle and read verses out of
the Bible. I didn't like it, 'cause I couldn't pronounce
some of the words."

"I see," she replied quietly, guiding her car along
the busy highway. *Don't get involved*, a voice whispered in her mind. *I'm already involved*, her conscience argued back. "Well, then, how would you like
to come to church with me on Sunday? The department you would visit has a terrific puppet show!"

"A puppet show?" he swung to look at her, his
eyes incredulous. "Why would they have something
like that in a *church*?"

She couldn't help laughing at his response. "The

52

teachers use puppets to tell the Bible stories. It's a lot more fun than sitting in a circle and reading. This way, you won't be embarrassed if you can't pronounce the words."

"Oh." He sank lower into his seat, his hands shoved deep into his pockets.

"Everyone loves the puppet show. I'll bet you would, too. Want me to come pick you up about 9:15 on Sunday morning?"

"Maybe," he nodded, squirming, "I like puppets."

"Great! Er, I'll ask your dad," she frowned, dreading another encounter with the defensive Simpson. Still, seeing the child in church, surrounded by caring adults and friendly children would be worth any unpleasantness she might encounter in asking his father for permission and she automatically drove faster in her eagerness to speak to Steve.

He greeted them at the door, his business suit rumpled, his tie loosened. The blue eyes were weary, haggard, underlined with dark circles. Casey wondered again what drove him so obsessively.

"Come in," Steve regarded his smiling son, then Casey, who wanted only to avoid his careful appraisal. He seemed to be attempting a friendly facade, but she sensed a stiff reserve where she was concerned.

Listening as Brad gave an animated account of monkeys and tigers and lions, Steve finally permitted a half-smile to curve his lips.

"Thanks for taking him. I can see this may be the main topic of conversation for days. Shall I have Martha put on some hot chocolate?" he asked belatedly.

"I can't stay," she shook her head. Even now, knowing the man had no interest in her beyond his son's welfare, Casey felt unsettled by his dark good looks and the intense blue gaze.

"I'm gonna have Martha fix me some hot choco-late!" Brad yelled. "See you Sunday, Casey."

With his parting words, he bounded off, his remark bringing a puzzled frown to Steve's face.

"Would you mind if I took Brad to Sunday school?" she asked quickly.

"I've already made plans for the two of us," he interrupted firmly, the voice brooking no argument.

"Well, maybe some other time," she mumbled, stunned by his abruptness.

When Steve refused to acknowledge her offer with any further comment, Casey was scarcely able to hide her irritation. She had a strong urge to tell him just what she thought of his method of child rearing, but she feared she would only make him angry again. There seemed to be nothing more to say.

"Well, good night." She turned for the door.

His hand reached out, the fingers gripping her arm. Even through the thick coat, his touch affected her strangely.

She turned, her brows lifted questioningly.

"Thanks again," he said softly, his gaze holding her captive for a speechless moment.

There was an unspoken message in the deep blue eyes, something akin to fear, that reached out to her, causing her to linger just when she would have pulled away.

"I loved having him with me," she responded, her cool facade melting beneath the liquid warmth of his eyes.

Slowly he released her, his hand sweeping forward to open the door. She walked out, unnerved by the awareness of his burning gaze trailing her down the steps, out the walk, back to the car.

She just didn't understand the man! What went on inside that complicated brain of his? His voice had told her one thing, while his eyes, his touch, had revealed something else entirely.

Back at her apartment, Casey pondered the tension between them. Strong vibrations crackled in the air when they were in the same room, so that, inevitably, they ended up snapping at each other, or glaring silently, unable to speak at all.

She had never experienced such intensity before. Although her experience with love had been limited to brief fascinations, she recognized the symptoms.

Casey plunged through the disorder of her apartment, diverting her confused thoughts to redecorating the place. She had moved in, months before, with the idea of completely renovating the plain rooms. But there had been no time.

Despite her efforts to occupy herself, one question kept nagging at her, interrupting her decision to forget the man. What did Steve Simpson *really* think of her? He kept watching her with an obvious fascination despite his abrupt speech and rude behavior.

Determined to put aside the events of the evening, Casey whirled into the bathroom and ran a tub of hot water. Nothing soothed her frayed nerves like a long soak. Adding a capful of bath oil, she returned to her bedroom, sorting through her chest of drawers for her favorite negligee in a silly attempt to reaffirm her femininity after Steve's cool indifference.

Except for the look . . . and the touch, she reminded herself.

She paused before her bedroom mirror, scrutinizing her reflection. Narrow shoulders, firm round breasts, tiny waist, flaring hips, legs that were too long for her petite frame. And she had dropped a few more pounds, she sighed, turning away.

Casey wondered if Steve sensed her attraction to him. She hoped not, since he apparently did not intend to reciprocate. Indeed, their relationship

55

seemed to be deteriorating before it had a chance to develop into something more than mutual concern for a small boy. First, she had put Steve off guard in that awful interview. Then he had interpreted her concern for Brad as criticism of his parenting, and he had bristled again. And now—the final straw—her conviction that Brad needed help beyond anything he could offer his son had pushed Steve too far.

Casey sank down on the bed, feeling a twinge of sympathy for the man. He seemed to have buried his heart with his wife, she thought sadly. Was his son only a heartbreaking reminder of her?

Beside her, the phone jangled on the nightstand and she jumped as though someone had touched her. Tossing her negligee onto the bed, she reached for the receiver, praying that it wasn't Ben with some ridiculous, late-night assignment.

"Casey, am I disturbing you?"

Steve! She gulped, amazed to hear his voice as if responding to her thoughts.

"No—" she replied, wondering why he should be calling so late.

He cleared his throat. She waited.

"Brad's really disappointed about missing that puppet show," he informed her.

She blinked, frowning at the sudden note of debate in his rich voice. *He probably uses that same tone in his closing argument to the jury*, she thought.

"I've changed my mind," he continued briskly. "If he wants to go, I don't object."

Objection overruled!

Her cool composure dissolved beneath sudden scalding anger. "Well, I certainly hope you don't *object*," she retorted. "Frankly, I should think you would appreciate someone taking an interest in your son!"

"Look, I'm getting tired of hearing about all the

56

mistakes I'm making with my son. Perhaps you don't realize it, but you have overreacted to a simple misunderstanding between a parent and a child. But not having children, you wouldn't understand," he reminded her emphatically.

"Oh, I understand," she echoed. "I understand much better than you think!"

Before she could phrase a final remark, he sharpened his attack, his voice cool and calculating. She could visualize him in his most polished courtroom performance.

"To be frank, I think your interest in us has exceeded the bounds of courtesy and has become downright offensive!"

"Really?" she snapped. "Then I'll assure you that I'll not interfere again. After Sunday, that is. I've made a promise to Brad, and I don't intend to break it. As for your son, I'm beginning to understand why he behaves the way he does. You have a heart of stone, Steve Simpson!"

Casey slammed the phone down and stood glaring at it. As her angry words echoed in her mind, she pressed cold fingers to her burning cheeks. What had come over her? Even if there was truth in her accusation, she should not have let him goad her into such a blatant attack.

She dragged herself into the bathroom and stared blankly at the tub of water. Her actions and words of the past moments had been anything but Christian. No wonder Steve doubted her good intentions. He hadn't seen anything different about her, nothing that set her apart from dozens of other people he knew. Certainly she hadn't exercised mercy or self-control or even simple kindness.

Marching back to the phone, she lifted her chin determinedly and dialed Steve's number quickly before she lost her resolve. Though she still felt less than contrite, Casey suspected the least she could do was go through the motions.

Steve's rich voice barked an angry hello, and she cleared her throat. "I'm sorry I behaved so badly a few minutes ago," she stated matter-of-factly. "What I said to you was thoughtless, cruel, and unnecessary. It seems I must ask you to forgive me again. Good-by." Then she replaced the receiver before another argument could erupt.

Going back into the bathroom, Casey added an extra supply of hot water and lowered herself into the steaming tub to soak away her anger.

Maybe now I can put the entire situation behind me, she thought, recalling her promise not to see or speak to Steve Simpson again after Sunday.

Somehow that thought did not bring the satisfaction she had anticipated.

CHAPTER 4

"Those puppets were really neat!" Brad shouted as Casey wheeled the little car out of the church parking lot. "I never had so much fun in Sunday school!"

Casey glanced across at him, a sad smile touching her lips. Dressed in a dark suit, with white shirt and striped tie, Brad was a handsome little fellow. She could imagine what a striking young man he would grow to become. Her gaze lingered on the rebellious strands of hair combed neatly in place before she turned back to the road, an ache filling her heart.

"I'm so glad you enjoyed it, Brad," she replied softly.

Her own Sunday school lesson had dealt with forgiveness, and she still considered it painfully ironic that the message in the Scripture seemed to apply so aptly to her present situation.

"I'm coming again next Sunday," Brad announced, his blue eyes glowing. "My—my new friends want me to come back, and I told them I'd be there."

Casey stared at his happy face and found herself

recalling the rebellious eyes, the downturned mouth, the drooping shoulders of the little boy who had shrunk back from her that first night at dinner. He seemed so different now, so happy and confident.

She turned back to the highway leading into the residential section, wondering what to do next. Perhaps Brad could handle the situation himself, she decided. He should be allowed to go to church if he wanted to. Surely his father could see the change in him. Perhaps Brad's enthusiasm would penetrate his father's doubts, making him see the importance of a religious background and the companionship of godly people.

As Brad toyed with the radio knob, she glanced into the car mirror, her gold-flecked gaze dropping to her brown woolen suit and dark floral blouse. Despite the sparkling sunshine of the unseasonably warm day, her mood had been dreary as she dressed this morning and she had chosen the most somber colors in her wardrobe.

She took a deep breath, hating the thought of not seeing Brad again. Rather than tell him, she decided it would be easier just to wave a cheery good-by and leave. Later, she could make excuses about her heavy work schedule.

A coward's way out, she realized, but there seemed to be no choice after Steve's hateful words.

As she slowed to turn into the driveway, Casey spotted Steve's tall figure in the center of the front lawn. He was dressed in casual clothes, a golf club swinging from his hand.

Carefully negotiating the turn in the drive, Casey planned to stop just long enough to deposit Brad.

"Hey, Dad!" Brad yelled. "The puppet show was super!"

"See you later, Brad," she said, resisting the urge to reach over and push him out so she could be gone.

Her eyes dared not stray to the approaching figure as she waited, her sandaled toe tapping an impatient rhythm on the accelerator, wishing Brad would hurry out of the car.

"Good morning," Steve leaned down, a wide smile revealing a row of perfect white teeth.

She couldn't have been more shocked if he had reached in and swatted her with his golf club!

"G-Good morning," she stammered, jerking her gaze back to the steering wheel.

"Going to play golf, Dad?" The sight of the golf club had mobilized Brad. "Because if you are, maybe I can go home with Casey."

"Just practicing my swing, son," Steve replied, reaching forward to tap Brad's shoulder affectionately. His congenial tone was almost as surprising as the broad smile.

"Well, see you, Brad," Casey forced her stiff mouth into the semblance of a smile as she glanced over her shoulder, making sure the driveway was clear before pulling the gear shift into reverse.

"Casey, I'd like to talk to you!" Steve had opened the door for Brad, offering him a friendly hand of assistance.

Casey swallowed hard, her gaze creeping across the front seat to the open door, meeting a pair of persistent blue eyes.

"We'd like you to stay for lunch—if you have no other plans, that is. In fact, I've already asked Martha to set a place for you," he added politely.

Was this the same man who had demanded in no uncertain terms that she clear out of his life?

She struggled to find her voice. "I really can't stay, but thank you," she added stiffly. "I—I have work to do."

The door opened wider and she felt the seat sinking beneath Steve's weight. Then the door slammed shut and she found herself face-to-face with the one man she was trying so diligently to avoid.

"Brad, run get your playclothes on," Steve suggested to Brad, who was lingering curiously by the door as though sensing the tension arcing between his father and his friend. "Hurry!" his dad prompted. "Martha has your favorite—lemon icebox pie!"

"Super!" Brad yelled, bounding off toward the house, his Sunday suit nearly splitting at the seams as he hurtled up the front steps.

Casey's spine stiffened in the momentary silence. The last thing she wanted was another verbal battle. She studied her hand, only half aware that her knuckles had turned white from her hard grip on the wheel.

"I'm *asking* you to stay for lunch, Casey."

It was more than a polite invitation. It was the genuine humility in his voice that drew her attention to his face. The dark hair and brows were offset by the rich blue of his eyes, and the hard line of jaw and chin were somehow softened by the quiet pleading in his level gaze.

Maybe it was the lesson of forgiveness from the Sunday school lesson. Maybe it was the irresistible little-boy look in Steve's eyes. Or maybe it was only because she simply couldn't help herself, but a warm smile curved her parted lips.

"Lunch is the very least I can do to make up for the terrible things I said to you. Please say you'll stay," he said huskily.

His urgent request sent her heart thudding against her rib cage as she blinked at him, feeling the impact of the virile man who sat uncomfortably near in the narrow front seat, dwarfing her little car with his size.

"I accept your apology if you'll overlook my temper tantrum as well," she said. "But there's no need to include lunch. I had planned on a sandwich at home."

"A sandwich!" he chuckled, the sound of his laughter doing strange things to her senses. "After herding Brad around, you need a T-bone steak!" His hand swept out, his fingers curving over hers. At his touch, every nerve ending responded to a deeper awareness of him. She struggled to keep her mind on what he was saying.

"Look, I'm aware of my faults, one of my worst being an overdose of pride. It's hard for me to admit my mistakes." The sincerity of his words was reflected in the darkening blue of his eyes. "I, more than anyone, am aware that Brad should have been in church long before now. I'm aware of a lot of things." Steve looked away from her, a deep sigh slipping from the full mouth as he stared straight ahead, his eyes narrowing. "It's just that, well, I hated having it pointed out so clearly. And I can't explain it," his gaze slid back to her, flicking over her thoughtfully, "but you have a very curious effect on me. I've been acting and reacting in irrational ways lately."

Their eyes locked, and Casey's mind reverted to her dizzied state whenever she was near Steve. Though she comprehended what he was saying, her senses seemed to have gone haywire from the effect of his hand on hers.

Her brown eyes widened, the gold flecks gleaming in their depths as she catalogued each feature of his face—the square, stubborn jaw, the slash of dark brow, the full curving lips. When she realized he was staring at her mouth with the same kind of fascination, she dragged her eyes away from his face, focusing blindly on the clean white lines of the Spanish-style house.

"Stay," he insisted softly.

She turned back to him, knowing she was lost

again. Deliberately she sought to break the seductive spell with light banter.

"How can I refuse?" she shrugged. "With canned soup for dinner last night and only juice for breakfast, there's no way I can pass up one of Martha's delicious meals." Her smile was tremulous.

"And this one is going to be free of tension," he promised, getting out of the car to come around and open her door.

The support of his hand on her arm sent a jangle along her nerve endings as she struggled to balance herself on her three-inch heels.

"You're so tiny," he laughed. "What is your height when you kick off those weapons?"

"Classified information," she teased back, enjoying the exchange of humor.

The meal was relaxed and carefree as Steve had promised, with Brad rambling on about every subject that popped into his head. Casey and Steve listened, often exchanging amused glances.

Even Martha joined them for lunch, pleased that her meal was being devoured in peace and obvious contentment. Still, Casey caught her appraising glance more than once, and she wondered about that. Martha seemed to be the one who had reservations about her.

As Brad finished off his pie, he swiped the napkin across his mouth, then shot an expectant glance toward Casey. "When are you taking me into the mountains like you promised?" he asked abruptly.

Casey stared at him, trying to remember when she had make that kind of commitment.

"Remember, at the circus you said you were going to Woodland Park sometime to see the aspens. I asked if I could go, and you said 'sure'."

"Brad, don't impose, son," Steve scolded, a frown darkening his face.

Casey's surprise at Brad's question was compound-ed by Steve's disapproving tone.

"That's okay," she replied with a reassuring smile. "I've been wanting to see the aspens for days, and since I have time off next Saturday, we could go then—if you want to."

"Whoopee!" Brad yelled. "*Just you and me!*"

Casey flinched at the thoughtlessness of his remark, the deliberate exclusion of his father. She moistened her lips, turning a reluctant glance toward Steve, wondering how to include him tactfully.

"Had you made plans for Brad?" she asked.

He shrugged. "Not really—"

"Would—you want to come with us, Steve?" she asked.

"I wanted just you and me to go!" Brad shouted in protest.

Casey's cheeks burned in embarrassment for Steve. How could the child be so cruel?

Her gaze flicked back to Brad, her lips parted to rectify the situation.

"I can't come," Steve replied, his tone clipped and brusque. "I've been promising an important client we'd play golf together."

Casey swallowed, unable to look at him, her gaze traveling instead to Martha's face. Martha was staring at Brad, a look of concern in her eyes. Then, glancing at Casey, another emotion crossed the woman's face. It was anger that flashed in her eyes before she turned away, busying herself with the dishes.

Casey was more confused than ever. She had counted on Martha as an ally, but it appeared that Martha either resented or disliked her.

"Well," Steve stook up, folding his napkin beside his plate. "I have some legal papers to go over in my study, so I'll leave the two of you to make your plans for Saturday." The polite smile scarcely concealed the edge in his voice. "Enjoyed it, Martha." The blue eyes returned to Casey, the old reserve filling their depths. "Have lunch with us again, Casey. Things seem to go better when you're here. Will you excuse me now?" His pain was evident.

"Of course," she nodded miserably. Was it obvious only to her that Brad's rejection was causing Steve to retreat once more to the only refuge he could be certain of—his work. And even that hadn't been certain lately, Casey reminded herself, thinking back to the case he had lost.

She lowered her gaze to her coffee cup, wondering how to deal with Brad.

Martha began to clear away the dishes, while Brad tugged at Casey's arm. "Wanna play a game of chess?"

She looked at him, unable to hide her irritation. "Brad, don't you realize that you hurt your father's feelings just now when you made it so clear you didn't want him to go along?"

The full bottom lip, a replica of his father's, extended in a threatening pout. "I don't care. Let him see how it feels to be left behind!"

"Brad, that isn't fair. Don't you remember what you learned from the puppets today? The Golden Rule?" she prompted as he stared blankly.

"Do unto others as you would have them do unto you," she reminded him, repeating the verse clearly.

He merely shrugged, his blue eyes flicking restlessly to the window. "Do you wanna play chess or not?" he asked, suddenly bored.

She stood up from the table, placing her napkin carefully across her plate. "No, I think I'll be going now."

"Why?" he asked crossly.

She turned to face him, aware that Martha was

watching curiously from a corner of the room, yet not hesitating to be honest with him about her feelings.

"Brad, I think you should know that I don't approve of the way you're acting. I can't pretend otherwise. If we're going to be friends, I won't put up with your behaving in a spoiled, selfish manner."

Her soft threat hung in the air, suddenly tense, as she forced her eyes not to stray from his shocked little face. She fully expected him to lash out at her, or, at the very least, to turn and run from the room.

To her surprise, he nodded.

"Awright," he said. "What time do you wanna go Saturday?"

She swallowed, trying to recover quickly. "How about nine o'clock?" she suggested, rewarding his agreeable manner with a warm smile. "Oh, and I'll pack us a picnic lunch," she added, winking at him.

"Okay," he brightened, walking beside her down the hall. At the front door his hand sneaked up, his fingers tugging at her wrist. "Do you want to see a picture of my mother?" he asked softly.

Casey was taken aback. She cleared her throat, wondering how to reply. Certainly Steve would not want a near stranger examining a picture of his late wife. And yet, she could not resist Brad's upturned face, the blue eyes wide and questioning. How could she refuse him?

"If you want me to," she nodded, following as he led her back down the hallway into a spacious room, which she recognized instantly as Steve's bedroom. She froze in the doorway, feeling like an intruder.

"He's in the study," Brad read her hesitation. "It's okay." He tugged at her arm.

"Brad, I really don't think—"

"See?" Brad interrupted, pointing toward one wall.

Lifting her eyes to a large, gilt-framed portrait, Casey found herself looking into the face of the striking beauty who had married Steve and given birth to Brad.

A cloud of black hair framed a heart-shaped face, the complexion flawless. The features were small and perfect; the mouth reserved, lifted in only a half-smile. Yet the enormous black eyes were captivating, tilting upward at the corners beneath a sweep of sooty lashes.

There was no denying that Scarlett was one of the most beautiful women Casey had ever seen. Almost unconsciously, her eyes scanned the room, inspecting the massive furnishing of a man's room, the lingering scent of Steve's aftershave tingling her nostrils.

Despite Martha's attempts at housekeeping, the room reflected a lived-in atmosphere. Books spilled over tables, a discarded jacket was flung over a chair, and dusty golf shoes sprawled in a corner. In her innocent sweep of the room, Casey's eyes fell on the small intimate photograph resting on the bedside table. It was a picture of Steve and Scarlett, with an infant Brad nestled between them. The couple was gazing into each other's eyes as though there was no one else in all the world.

Casey turned away, sick at heart, unable to distin-guish whether her pain was born out of sadness for the deep love Steve had lost, or if the picture merely reaffirmed what she had already feared—that no woman could ever hope to replace the beautiful Scarlet in Steve's heart and mind.

"She was a lovely lady, Brad," she said, taking a deep breath. "I know you and your father miss her very much."

Her gaze dropped to his upturned face, expecting his eyes to be clouded with tears. To her surprise, he merely seemed to be interested in her reaction.

She frowned, resisting the impulse to turn and tiptoe out of the room.

"I really must go, Brad," she said, forcing herself to walk normally.

"Don't forget about Saturday," Brad squeezed her hand as they reached the front door.

"No," she looked down at him, a new sympathy for the boy and the man clouding her vision. "No, honey, I won't."

Casey found herself looking forward to her Saturday with Brad. During her busy week, his nightly telephone calls eased the tension of her hectic work days, as she lost herself in the little boy's idle chatter.

On Saturday morning she hopped out of bed early, dressing warmly in woolen socks and hiking boots, heavy jeans, blouse and cardigan. Throwing her hooded parka around her shoulders, she dashed off to the market, adding potato chips and canned pop to the sandwiches and homemade chocolate chip cookies.

When she wheeled into the Simpson drive and got out, casting a thankful glance toward cool sunny skies, she was greeted at the front door by a worried Steve.

"Casey, I've been trying to call you." His gaze flicked down her picnic clothes as he opened the front door.

"Something wrong?" she asked, looking about for Brad.

"Brad got up with a stomach ache," Steve sighed. "I didn't want to call too early, thinking you might sleep in on your day off." His tone was apologetic.

"Oh, I dressed early and went to the market," she explained.

"Come on back to the kitchen." His hand slipped easily around her shoulder, guiding her down the hall to the back of the house. "There's fresh coffee."

Casey tried to ignore her creeping disappointment.

69

Picnicking alone was no fun. But Brad's illness was of more immediate concern.

"I hope it's nothing serious with Brad," she sat down at the kitchen table, removing her coat and placing it on the back of the oaken chair.

"He was fine last night." Steve filled two mugs with coffee and returned to the table. "As a matter of fact, I have to admit to you that Brad is happier than he's been in a long time. I think you're responsible," he added, looking across at her thoughtfully.

"Really, I haven't done anything," she replied lightly, unwilling to focus attention on herself.

She thought back to the Sunday before, when Steve had tried to hide his wounded pride in being deliberately excluded from their little outing.

"Speaking of Brad's state of mind, Martha tells me you put him in his place after I left the room, and that he accepted what you had to say without a fight." Steve turned back to his coffee, avoiding her quick glance. "You may have been right about the counselor," his voice was low and husky. "Brad's a very bright boy, and I think he outsmarts Martha and me most of the time. I've probably been too easy on him." he added, dropping his head to study the contents of his coffee cup.

Casey studied the rugged profile, her heart going out to him. With his face averted, she allowed herself a surreptitious appraisal, noting his lean frame in the casual jeans and crew neck sweater, the strong set of his shoulders, the proud tilt of his dark head. He was a man she could easily love, she realized with a pang. Would that be so bad? she wondered, her gaze shifting nervously to her hands, folded on the neat, red-checkered cloth.

Then she remembered Scarlett.

". . . and it may be my fault," Steve was saying, looking at her as though he expected a response.

70

"I beg your pardon?" She looked at him inquiringly, forcibly rejecting the mental image of the lovely, dark-haired Scarlett.

"I said, I think I understand the stomach ache. It may be my fault."

Her eyes scanned his face, trying to comprehend his meaning.

"We watched a television program together and I confess to popping at least a gallon of popcorn, heavily salted and slightly over-buttered!"

"Oh, no wonder!" Casey laughed as he grinned impishly, the blue eyes gleaming.

"I guess you've already prepared the lunch," Steve ventured, sipping his coffee.

"Well, yes. But I'll just go on alone," she decided aloud. "This will be my only chance to see the aspens at their prime."

Her cheerful voice belied the cloud of disappointment within. On her lonely excursion into the mountains last fall, she had discovered that such glorious beauty was meant to be shared.

"Would you mind if I tagged along?"

Startled by the unexpected suggestion, Casey's brown eyes shot to his face. Before she had time to consider the idea, he continued smoothly.

"Martha will be here with Brad. Since he isn't running a fever, I think it's safe for me to leave. In fact, he suggested it!"

"He did?" Her eyes widened, wondering what had prompted the change of heart.

"Well, since you'd gone to the trouble to pack a lunch for two—" he added defensively.

"You're right," she nodded, remembering his overdose of pride. "And if I'm left alone with a dozen chocolate chip cookies, *I'll* be the one with the stomach ache. What about your day at the golf course?"

He shrugged. "Today—I'd rather go to the mountains! Want more coffee while I grab a jacket?"

"No, thanks. Is Brad asleep?" She glanced toward the quiet hallway.

"Yes. He went back to bed after I agreed to offer myself as a replacement. Sure you don't mind?" he asked, hesitating in the doorway.

"Of course not! I'll be glad to have you," she replied honestly.

"Then I'll knock on Martha's door and tell her we're leaving," he called over his shoulder.

Casey sat at the table, staring at her empty mug. What a strange turn of events! She had managed to convince herself, after seeing the picture of Scarlett and remembering Steve's reaction to her name, that he was not ready for a relationship. Now he had just invited himself to spend a day with her in the mountains—and *Brad had suggested it*! Yet, recalling his words on Sunday—*"you have a very curious effect on me. . . .I've been acting and reacting in irrational ways lately. . ."* she found herself hoping again that Steve might be interested in her.

He was the kind of man who would keep life exciting and fast-paced. There were so many facets of his personality. While he was intelligent, curious, aggressive and ambitious to a fault, he could also be gentle, considerate, understanding and . . . unpredictable!

A day in the mountains would probably prove to be a very interesting experience! An expression of amusement tilted the corners of her mouth as she thought of Steve munching a peanut butter sandwich. But since this had been planned as a young boy's outing, she reasoned, he would just have to suffer the consequences!

Casey suppressed a shiver of excitement in anticipation of what the day would bring.

CHAPTER 5

STEVE APPEARED IN the doorway, a navy parka tossed carelessly over his shoulder, a pleasant sparkle in his blue eyes.

"Ready?" he asked. "Since I have a jeep parked in the garage, one that's seen little use I might add, what do you say to our taking it? A four-wheel-drive might be more practical if we're going to be climbing mountain roads."

"Sounds like a good idea." Casey stood up, tugging on her jacket.

"Then I'll just back the jeep, and we can transfer your things."

She followed him out the back door, her steps quickening at the idea of having a handsome chauffeur do the driving while she took in the glorious autumn scenery.

After they had left the sleepy neighborhood behind, Casey leaned back in the seat and concentrated on the golden aspen groves along the foothills.

"I haven't done anything like this in a long time,"

Steve admitted, gripping the wheel. "I suddenly feel like a kid playing hooky from school!"

Casey laughed at his carefree exuberance, studying his profile silhouetted against the passing scenery. The lean features were relaxed, the brows free of the deep furrow hovering between their dark arch. The lips, no longer drawn in a tight strained line, curved sensually over white teeth.

Her gaze flew back to the winding road as she forced her thoughts to safer channels. Yes, Steve was an extremely attractive man, but she could only hope for a pleasant friendship with him—nothing more. And considering their stormy beginning, it would be no small miracle if they could simply be civil to each other for the remainder of the day.

The hum of the jeep pulling the gradual incline up Ute Pass droned through their companionable silence as they passed tourist shops advertising handmade leather items, unique rocks, gems, and local art.

"How long have you been in Colorado?" Steve asked conversationally.

"I came soon after graduate school," she smiled, remembering. "I vacationed here with my parents during some of the humid Texas summers and I promised myself that someday I'd take full advantage of this wonderful mountain air. And you?" she asked, shifting in her seat to look across at him.

"Born and raised here, with only a brief stint back East for law school. I learned then how fortunate I was to be a Coloradan." His blue gaze swung upward to Pikes Peak's snowy crown. "I can't imagine starting a day without a view of that mountain and a chestful of pure dry air!"

"I know," she laughed, the glow of their new companionship warming her. "Does your family live here now?"

"My parents have retired and are living down in

Phoenix. Mom grew tired of the long winters. My sister is married and living in Denver. Now there's just me," he grinned at her. "And you probably come from a large family—several brothers, at least."

"One brother, and thank you for not suggesting that I'm the baby, which I am. Why did you guess I might have brothers?"

"Your patience with Brad and me. Obviously, I'm not the easy-going type, but I'm working hard at improving." His broad shoulders lifted in a deep sigh. "Casey, I appreciate your overlooking my odd behavior at times. Not everyone would be able to do that." His voice drifted away thoughtfully, and she wondered if he was thinking of Scarlett. "And thanks for taking Brad to church. He's talked about that puppet show all week."

Casey smiled, wondering whether to pursue the topic or let it go, remembering his sensitivity to outside interference. She decided to take the chance.

"I'll be glad to take him any Sunday," she offered pleasantly.

He stared ahead in silence, dark brows lowered formidably. Wheeling the jeep into the sleepy little village of Woodland Park, Steve glanced toward her and asked in an obvious change of subject, "Do you have a favorite picnic area up here?"

She regarded the quaint western town, then suggested, "What about Manitou Lake?"

"Fine." He swung the jeep into a right turn at the intersection, driving east past dense pine-and-spruce groves, interspersed with aspens in various shades of gold.

Casey watched the passing scenery, a relaxed sigh slipping from her lips as she gazed out at the mountain valley, rimmed by an emerald lake, sparkling in the noonday sun. She was determined to be a pleasant traveling companion, not pushing any subject too far, or goading Steve into a dark mood. He needed this day of relaxation as much as she—perhaps more.

He turned into the main gate leading to the picnic site, winding past couples and families occupying tables, and on to a secluded spot beside the lake.

"Well, let's see what surprises you have in that picnic basket," he grinned across at her, reaching into the back seat for the wicker hamper.

Casey climbed out of the jeep, wondering if she should apologize for the meager fare now that the mountain air had whetted their appetites. She watched as he placed the basket on a table, then reached for a fallen pine branch to whisk the debris from the table.

Casey busied herself hauling out paper plates and cups, large cans of cola, then arranging the potato chips and plastic-wrapped sandwiches. By the time she reached the container of cookies, she could no longer suppress a giggle.

"What's so funny?" he asked suspiciously, slapping his dusty hands on his Levi-clad thighs.

"How does peanut butter and grape jelly strike you?" She raised mischievous eyes to him, awaiting his reaction.

"Strikes me as the perfect picnic sandwich." He accepted one eagerly, then swung his long legs over the bench and sat down, his interested gaze flicking over the remainder of the lunch. "Brad shouldn't be missing this. He complains about Martha's fancy casseroles. Mmmm," he took a big bite, "I can honestly say this is the best sandwich I've ever tasted!"

"Oh, come on!" Casey laughed, pouring the cola into cups and extending one to him. "I'm much too content today to flare into my usual defense." She sat down opposite him, tearing into the large bag of chips.

"I mean it," he looked across at her. "A day in the

company of a lovely lady and a mountain view that defies description—why, a charcoaled T-bone wouldn't taste any better."

"Oh, I doubt that," she laughed. "Since I've been too weary for an evening on the town, and since I would never attempt to grill a steak myself, I've almost forgotten how a good steak tastes."

He reached for his drink, glancing at her thoughtfully. "Then, in return for the tasty lunch, I intend to see that you have the best steak in town on your next free evening? Or do you ever *have* a free evening?"

"For a steak dinner, I'll *make* a free evening," she promised.

When they finished the lunch, Steve stood up, taking her hand. "Let's take a walk. All this food could make us lazy if we don't stretch our legs."

"All this food?" she repeated, laughing, as her fingers laced through his.

She stared at the path before them, littered with pine needles and an occasional pop can, trying to collect her thoughts. Steve seemed so different today, his good mood obvious once he left the cares of his workaday world behind. Could she possibly hope . . .

Casey allowed her eyes to drift upward to the spiraling blue spruce, and studied the shaft of golden sunlight filtering through the heavy branches. It was unfair to read anything beyond friendship in Steve's actions, yet she had always believed that the best relationships began with deep friendship.

They were crossing the wooden bridge that spanned the lake now, and paused in the middle to watch a distant fisherman as he cast his line in search of a hungry trout.

"I hope Brad is feeling better," Casey said with concern as she leaned against the wooden railing.

"I'm sure he is," Steve looked down at her. "I'm a little suspicious of his motives today, anyway."

"What do you mean?" she asked, her brows arched quizzically.

"He thinks you're about the greatest person he's ever met. I hope you won't take offense if I suggest that he may have been playing Cupid."

Surprise widened her brown eyes before realization dawned, and she looked back at the lake, slightly embarrassed. Was Brad faking the stomach ache? And the curious expression on his face when he had shown his mother's picture—was he testing her then?

"I'm not offended at all," she replied quietly, watching as the fisherman reeled in a wiggling trout. "But—" she broke off, unable to voice her doubts.

"But what?" he asked, leaning on one elbow against the railing, the blue eyes fixed on her face.

"I have the impression there is no room in your life for another woman." She turned to face him squarely.

"There hasn't been—before," he replied quietly. "I've been too preoccupied with work. But," he looked into the distance, his eyes seeking the fisherman once more, "work shouldn't dominate a person's life. When I first began my practice of law, it was a matter of pride to see how many cases I could win. Then when Scarlett died," his voice lowered and Casey tensed in response, "I used my work as an escape. By that time Brad and I had drifted apart and I didn't know how to reach him. Work was an escape from *that* dilemma, too. But now," he turned to face her, his eyes brightening with hope, "I've been reassessing my priorities. Brad will come first from now on."

Casey touched his arm. "Steve, I'm so glad!" Sobering, she continued. "I'm sorry about the Holcomb case, particularly if your client was innocent."

He shrugged. "Maybe he wasn't. The Holcombs

78

have been friends of mine for years. When Ted Holcomb asked me to take his son's case, I could hardly refuse. I had doubts—" his voice trailed away as he looked down at her, a grin tugging at his mouth. "Hey, here we are discussing business, and that's strictly against the rules today."

"I agree," she laughed. "Shall we walk back and sample my homemade cookies, which may have turned to stones by now?"

"Ah," he took her arm, guiding her across the planked bridge, "homemade cookies. Somehow I hadn't pictured you as the domestic type."

"I resent that." She made a pretense of being offended, then gave him a sly grin. "Even if you have hit upon the truth, as the old saying goes, the truth hurts!"

"You haven't time," he defended, "and there may have been no need for domesticity. Or has there?"

She shrugged, not following his line of reasoning until they had reached the picnic table. Then, looking across at him in sudden understanding, she smiled. "I've never been married, if that's what you mean."

"Not even a commitment?"

"Not even a commitment," she replied, removing the lid and extending the container of cookies to him.

"I find that hard to believe," he shook his head, the blue eyes pensive.

"Careful," she nodded toward the cookies. "They may be lethal."

"Mmmm." He munched one and grinned. "I take back what I said about your not being domestic."

She shook her head, busying herself cleaning up the plates and cups. "I could use a few cooking lessons," she admitted, "although my mother did her best. It's just that I was always busy with school activities, and then after school I came here."

"You seem to have managed your life just fine."

He looked out across the lake, the blue eyes darkening.

"Well, I've been fortunate, and I've worked hard," she said. "But mainly I've relied on God for guidance in making important decisions."

"I see," he turned to her thoughtfully, apparently weighing her words.

She thought of Steve's life in contrast, a sharp ache twisting through her. Searching for the right comment to fill the awkward silence, Casey found herself unable to relate to the tragedy in his life.

Steve rose, interrupting the sudden melancholy of the mood, "Well, if you're ready, I have a few favorite jeep trails I'd like to show you."

"Fine," Casey smiled at him, eager to leave behind the dark cloud that threatened to dampen their enjoyment of the day.

The afternoon slipped pleasantly away as they jeeped the high mountain roads, lingering at one scenic overlook to gasp at the beauty of a hillside, liquid gold in the brilliant sunlight.

Casey sighed. "Whenever I look upon such beauty, I cannot understand how anyone could doubt the existence of God."

"Belief is one thing. Living up to His expectations is something else, I've found."

"His or yours?" she asked boldly. "I have a feeling you set awfully high standards for yourself, Steve Simpson. No one is perfect!"

"Hmmm," he pursed his lips, staring down at her. "You're beginning to penetrate that hardened lump in the center of my chest, sometimes known as a heart. Why?" he gazed at her curiously. "What is there about you that makes me want to be a better person?"

"I have no idea," she laughed. "Maybe you just *want* to be a better person."

"Whatever the reason, I like being with you,

Casey. I think you're very good for me," he said, as his dark head bent to her bright one, and his lips brushed her forehead.

Just like my brother would do, Casey thought, mildly amused. That was probably the extent of Steve's feelings for her, too. A sort of protective companionship. Nothing serious. Nothing permanent.

She shivered into her jacket. "I suddenly feel cold." She avoided his sidelong glance. "Shall we head back?"

"I guess it's that time." Steve glanced at his watch reluctantly.

Earlier, they had made short work of reloading the jeep, having disposed of most of the food. But Casey kept the tin of cookies in the front seat—ready for munching on the way home and for filling any uncomfortable silences between them.

Back in Colorado Springs, Steve reached across to grasp Casey's hand. "Thanks for the best day I've spent in . . . " he shrugged, "I can't remember when. Won't you come in?" he asked, guiding the dusty jeep back into the garage.

"For only a minute. I'd like to see Brad," she smiled, wondering if he was really sick, or if, as Steve suggested, he had merely been playing Cupid. She couldn't imagine his missing out on a day in the mountains for any reason, but then she was only beginning to glimpse Brad's resourcefulness.

They found him in the den, nestled in a mound of sofa pillows, absorbed in a television mystery.

"Brad, how do you feel?" Casey asked anxiously, leaning down to pat his shoulder.

"Fine." The blue eyes darted over her face, then his father's. "Did you two have a good time?" he asked eagerly.

81

Casey straightened, avoiding Steve's knowing glance, their suspicions confirmed.

"A great time! Wish you could have been with us," Steve replied.

"There was a double feature on the afternoon showtime," Brad yawned. "Frankie came over to watch it with me. Martha made us some fudge."

"Aha! So your stomach is *lots* better." Steve grinned at Casey.

"Oh, Miss Green," Martha interrupted, "your answering service has been trying to reach you. You're to telephone the station immediately!"

"Thank you. May I use the telephone in your study?" she asked Steve.

"Of course." He led the way down the hall, casting a concerned glance at her as he opened the door and flicked on a light.

When Casey called the station, she learned that one of the anchors had suffered a light heart attack and that she had been drafted to replace him temporarily.

"Have you ever anchored the news before?" Steve asked as she repeated the message.

"Actually, I'll be co-anchoring, and yes, I've done it once or twice. Each time I was a bundle of nerves," she confessed with a sigh. "I don't feel comfortable sitting before a camera, reading news from a Teleprompter. I prefer to be out there where it's happening! Well," her glance skimmed the interested faces, "I'd better get home and rest up for tomorrow."

"Does this mean we can't go to Sunday school?" Brad grumbled.

Casey bit her lip, remembering. "I'm sorry, Brad. I don't like having to work on Sunday, but this is an emergency."

Steve remained silent in the background.

"Well, good night." Casey waved to Brad and Martha, then turned to Steve.

"I'll walk you to your car," he offered, stretching his legs to keep up with her hurried pace down the hall.

"Steve, this has been a marvelous day," she smiled up at him as they stepped out into the chill night air.

"I know," he looked at her significantly. "I'm not ready for it to end."

As they walked in silence to her car, Steve's hand reached out for hers, and it seemed natural that their fingers should intertwine. Casey had discovered another Steve today—a man who was gentle and caring and thoughtful. Even his attitude toward Brad seemed more relaxed and tolerant. This new discovery had broken down her defenses, and she deeply regretted having to say good night.

She glanced up at the moonlight filtering through the dark pines, cloaking them in a silvery haze. Was it the moonlight, she wondered, or the man beside her that set this night, this moment apart from all others of her life? Her senses were finely attuned to Steve's every movement and to her own quickening pulse.

As Steve leaned forward to open the door of her car, he paused, reaching for her instead. Strong hands gripped her shoulders, drawing her close. Breathlessly she watched as he lowered his dark head, closing the distance between them. Casey was unable to move. Not that she wanted to. Her hands were resting lightly on his chest, fingers flattened against the nubby warmth of his sweater as his lips found hers. The kiss could have lasted a second or an eternity, for Casey was swept beyond all awareness of time and space.

When finally Steve lifted his head, his eyes searched hers as if trying to discern her thoughts. "It's cold out here," he said huskily. "I shouldn't keep you."

She wanted to protest, but her voice failed her. She

could only stare, entranced, into those mystical blue eyes, her pulse racing dangerously.

Men had pursued her before, but none had ever possessed her heart. Certainly no man had ever affected her the way Steve did.

He seemed to sense her vulnerability. Tenderly he cupped her chin in his hand. This time, when his mouth moved over the soft contours of her lips, the kiss became more urgent. Casey felt shaken to the depth of her being. Frightened by the intensity of her response, she pulled away, averting her eyes.

"I really must go," she said, hopping into the cold front seat. "Good night," she called over her shoulder, fumbling with the car keys, then starting the engine.

"I'll call," he promised, closing her door.

She nodded, backing the car out of the driveway, then remembering that she hadn't turned on the headlights.

"I'm as giddy as a sixteen-year-old," she sighed, screeching the tires as she roared off through the quiet neighborhood.

I'm falling in love with him, she thought, suddenly panicky. She wasn't sure she was ready for this, and in her hectic work schedule there hardly seemed time for such an involvement.

But love was no respecter of persons, she knew. One did not make a random selection, then proceed to fall in love. There had to be a special magic between two people after the friendship. The magic had been there from the beginning, she realized with a flash of perception. From the very first moment she saw him on the courthouse steps, Casey had been undeniably, irrevocably drawn to Steve.

Nervously she reached forward to flick the radio dial, tuning in an easy-listening stereo station. As a familiar love song drifted over the air waves, she found herself humming the tune, recalling that wonderful moment in Steve's arms.

She had always prayed that God would send her the right person, a man whose love would lead to a happy marriage. But she had not expected that man to be a widower, to have already loved someone deeply. And what about Steve's faith? By his own admission that, too, was in question.

But she was losing her heart to this man, and there seemed to be nothing she could do to prevent it.

CHAPTER 6

CASEY SAT AT her desk, scanning a news report describing an avalanche in the San Juan mountains. She frowned. She had attributed her dwindling concentration to stress and lack of sleep, but as Steve drifted through her thoughts again, she realized the source of her frustration.

She propped her elbows on her desk, her chin thrust in her palms. Their last telephone conversation had been interrupted as Ben waved a note under her nose and Steve's secretary stood waiting to take dictation. They were both too busy for a relationship—why couldn't they face that fact?

"Can you speak to the Rotary Club on Thursday?" Mona burst into her line of vision, her head inclined to penetrate Casey's wandering gaze.

"I . . . what?" Casey frowned. "Oh, not this week. And, Mona, I'd rather not tackle *any* speaking engagements for a while—at least not while I'm filling in for Hal. Get someone else, will you?"

"Better be ready," Mona trilled. "We're receiving

lots of favorable calls about your replacing Hal. In fact, dear ol' Hal better hurry out of that hospital soon, or he just may be *permanently* replaced by a popular little blonde!''

Casey's brows lifted in surprise. "Really, Mona, I think you're exaggerating. Hal's been with the station for years.''

"All I know is what I hear,'' Mona teased, her words trailing across the newsroom.

Casey smiled after her, appreciating the vivacious secretary's efforts to lift her gloomy mood.

The telephone rang, and Steve's deep voice on the other end brought her upright, her spirits soaring at the sound.

"Do you think there's a chance we could meet for dinner?'' he asked, the tentative question a reminder that she had been forced to refuse the past three invitations.

She thrust her chin forward with a brisk nod. "I'm going to collect on that steak if it's the last thing I do! No matter *what* comes up, I'll meet you after the newscast this evening,'' she promised.

"Great! Spoken like a woman of her word. I'm going to depend on that.'' His voice lowered, the rich tone warming her senses, filling her with a deep need to see him again.

They decided on the restaurant, named the hour, then Casey turned back to her work, an impish grin tilting her lips. She attacked the report with new determination, viewing the task as a means to an end—the reward being dinner with Steve.

He was waiting for her in the stone foyer of an elegant restaurant where candles flickered at cozy linen-covered tables, and the muted voices of dinner companions blended with the relaxing atmosphere.

"Hope I'm not late," she called breathlessly, as he helped her out of her coat, his touch almost a caress.

"You're just in time—and much prettier in person than on the tube!" Steve's hand pressed the small of her back, guiding her across the crowded dining room to a secluded table in the corner.

He pulled out a velvet-cushioned chair. Casey couldn't see the blue gaze that lingered on the soft cloud of golden hair swirling about her shoulders. Then he seated herself opposite her and smiled. "If you'd like, I'll order for us. Since this is my favorite restaurant, I take pride in being an authority on their food."

"Terrific! Not having to make one single decision on my own is pure luxury. How's Brad?"

"He's fine. His grades improved this six weeks, and he's been wearing an extra-wide grin for days, as though he's masterminding some interesting little scheme."

Casey laughed softly, her eyes drinking in every feature of Steve's masculine face, then scanning his pin-striped suit and silk shirt. There was an easy grace about him, complementing everything he wore, from business clothes to faded jeans.

"I've missed you." His hand slipped across the table, pressing her cold fingers. "Much more than you could know."

"I've missed you, too," she admitted, her straightforward manner precluding any attempt to mask her feelings.

"Can we make plans for the weekend?" Steve asked anxiously. "And please don't say Hal is still sick. I'm considering bribing his doctors for a miracle cure! I *have* to see you," he finished, his hand squeezing hers.

A waiter cleared his throat, placing their spinach salad before them.

"I would *love* having a day off," Casey sighed wistfully, "but just now I can't say when. I'm beginning to dream about political conventions and robberies and ... *food*." She speared her salad eagerly.

"I'll be returning to court next week," he reminded her, "which means I'll be tied up for days with my client."

"Tell me about the case," she glanced up with interest.

"A child custody suit—one that's sure to get nasty before it's over."

"Oh? Which parent are you representing?"

"The mother. She's agreed to joint custody, but the guy is so bitter that he's demanding full custody. He's trying to default her character through phony witnesses. I won't allow that kind of mistreatment." The blue eyes hardened. "She's a good woman who committed herself to marriage and family. She deserves better."

They watched silently as the waiter appeared with sizzling steaks on pewter platters, the break in conversation providing Casey with an opportunity to weigh his words. Steve's obvious respect for his client caused her to question her own goals. Was this the kind of woman Steve preferred—someone committed to keeping a home, with no outside interests? Well, Casey Green was certainly a far cry from that sweet image! Why, she wasn't even domestic, although she'd always longed to experiment with interior decorating. But her cooking was a joke and her housekeeping was pathetic.

Her appetite began to wane, the meat thickening in her mouth. He was right, of course. What Steve needed was a sweet little homebody to care for him and his young son. How on earth had she allowed herself to become involved with someone who needed a woman the exact opposite of herself?

"Scarlett and I were not the happy couple most people believed we were," Steve admitted softly, the confession widening Casey's eyes in surprise. "She was a very successful model. I don't want to speak ill of her now," his blue eyes darkened, "but Brad and I were not her main interest in life. Her work was. She often flew to New York or Los Angeles to tape television commercials. If it hadn't been for Martha—" his voice trailed away, a dark frown creasing his brow.

Casey stared at him, sensing his pain, and the pain of a young boy who needed the love of both parents. She could understand Brad's anger and frustration, his desperate need for attention. Was he now centering his hopes on *her*? That would be a mistake, considering the hectic pace of her own job. And her almost overnight success as co-anchor promised that quality time with Steve—and with Brad—would be even more scarce in the future. She sat staring into space, this new revelation overshadowing her recent happiness.

She caught Steve's curious gaze on her, reminding her that she had lapsed into a worried silence, unable to take part in a conversation that left her reeling with the futility of their relationship.

"Well, how did the conversation become so morbid?" he asked, smiling.

"I think you were explaining your commitment to your client," she reminded him. But the subject of the upcoming trial was only secondary, Casey knew. What she had heard, between the lines, was the sound of another ugly barrier being erected between them. This time, it was an age-old issue—the dilemma of career vs. marriage and family.

90

"Oh, yes. Well, I trust that justice will prevail," he quipped, in a half-hearted attempt at humor.

Casey tried to concentrate on her meal, hoping to relish some enjoyment from the tasty food, but she discovered that her appetite had dwindled with each bite.

"Well," she took a deep breath, forcing herself to say the words she hated, "as much as I enjoyed this steak, I do have a busy day tomorrow."

"All right—if you feel you really must go." Steve stood, assisting Casey from the chair.

"Thanks for a lovely meal," she smiled at him as they crossed the dining room. "And say hello to Brad for me."

"Casey," his hand lingered on her elbow as they walked out the front door, "somehow I feel that an invisible wall went up between us back there." He nodded over his shoulder toward the dining room.

"I—I'm just tired, Steve. Good night." Her sharp heels echoed across the quiet parking lot as she hurried away, aware that she had evaded his question, leaving him to wonder.

But didn't Steve recognize the truth? Wasn't it as glaringly apparent to him as to her? Otherwise, why had he even broached the subject, if not to drop a less than subtle hint about his choice of a woman—one who tied on the apron strings and puttered around the kitchen all day, waiting for her man to come home!

Could I do that? she wondered, sinking into the car seat, startled by the fact that she was even considering the thought.

No, of course not! She cranked the engine of her car and wheeled out of the parking lot.

Dear God, I don't see an answer to this, she thought wearily. *How can we build a relationship when we are poles apart?* The answer seemed heart-

91

breakingly obvious. Hopelessly she wound through the dark streets back to her lonely apartment.

"With bone structure like yours, today's job is a snap!" smiled Suzy, the make-up artist, as she whisked rose blusher onto Casey's smooth skin.

"You're just talented," Casey countered, studying her new look. The bold eye make-up made her brown eyes appear deep and mysterious, while her blond hair, swept back from her face, revealed more prominently her classic features. Casey felt stiff and unnatural, but she remained silent, deciding to trust the opinion of experts.

Her bewildered gaze dropped to the stark navy suit, the bright red bow of her silk blouse adding a splash of color to offset her otherwise tailored appearance. And yet the wardrobe consultant had suggested the suit, explaining her need to look older.

"Why do I want to look *older*?" Casey had joked.

"Because you'd have a hard time convincing anyone you're over twenty-one and thus capable of handling such an important job," came the caustic reply.

Now the possibility of going before a television camera each evening, looking far too glamorous and sophisticated for her own taste, made her grimace.

"I don't know why I let myself be talked into this audition," she mumbled, leaning back in the chair with a regretful sigh. "If Hal isn't returning to work, there are other people more qualified."

"I hear you're the favorite," Suzy whispered. "Besides, you mustn't resist opportunity when it knocks! You know the old saying. It may never come again," she reminded her as she seized a can of hair spray and enveloped Casey in a cloud of mist.

"Casey? You're on next. Come on up to the control

92

room." A technician popped through the door, then disappeared just as quickly.

"Thanks, Suzy," Casey stood up, taking one last look in the mirror and shaking her head in dismay.

"Good luck," Suzy called after her as Casey walked out into the long corridor leading to the stairway.

As Casey climbed the narrow flight of stairs, her heart began to hammer, not in fear, but in response to the step she was taking. *Is this really what I want? To be a television anchor?* she frowned, as she opened the door and slipped quietly into the control room.

Squinting against the dimness as the technicians adjusted controls, she peered through the glass window to the stage below where a well-known anchor from a Denver station sat reading a script to Mr. Rosenthall, the general manager, who was sitting in the front row.

"You're next," someone whispered, and she nodded in reply, hurrying out the door and down the back steps to the stage.

Casey stood in the background, analyzing the smooth delivery of the man as he finished his last line and glanced expectantly toward the front row. He was answered with a brisk nod before Casey was waved onto the stage.

She squared her shoulders and walked quickly to the small rectangular platform that served as the news desk. Seating herself, she scanned the two typewritten sheets as she cleared her throat.

"You know what to do," one technician whispered. "Just flash that all-American smile!"

Given the nod, she began to read, her voice ringing across the quiet stage as she directed her attention to Camera One, only vaguely aware of Mr. Rosenthall, leaning forward in the front row. After she had finished, she blinked into the bright lights, waiting for a response. When there was none, she stood to leave.

"Miss Green?"

She paused, turning back.

"Well-done." The silver-haired Rosenthall strolled up to her, his hand extended.

"Thank you," she nodded, gripping his large hand.

"And may I say you've done a splendid job in replacing Hal on such short notice! You're aware of the ratings?"

"Yes," she replied modestly, taking in the distinguished man who controlled the hiring and firing of employees with a mere nod of his silvery head.

"You don't sound as Texan as we had expected. Normally, we're sensitive about accents, but the public seems quite taken with yours! In fact, you've brought a bit of a new dimension to television newscasting."

She shifted uncomfortably, wondering how to reply. She quickly decided to center the conversation on Hal, making a complimentary remark about his popularity as news anchor. Soon, a secretary was waving a telephone toward the older man, and she breathed a deep sigh of relief when he nodded to her and hurried off.

She returned to her desk, filled with an uneasiness she couldn't define. She had been staring blankly at a stack of telephone messages when someone tapped her on the shoulder and pointed to her ringing telephone. She dived for it, self-consciously aware that she was the object of a few questioning stares.

As soon as she spoke a quick hello, Brad's eager reply filled her ears, bringing a smile of pleasure to her tense lips.

"Brad, I'm glad to hear from you!" she exclaimed, cradling the phone against her shoulder while she flipped idly through the telephone messages. "I've missed our conversations."

"You're always too busy," he complained loudly. "Are we going to Sunday school this Sunday?"

"I'm sorry, honey," she sighed. "I still have not been replaced on Sundays." She pushed the messages aside, her brows furrowed in a worried frown.

"You told me people shouldn't miss Sunday school every week, remember?"

She nodded, one hand lifted to press her throbbing forehead. "I know, but I have to work. Maybe we can plan something later."

The chances of planning *anything* were slim, but she hadn't the heart to dash his hopes. Not yet.

"I . . . miss . . . you, Casey!" Brad cried, his words sweetly poignant.

Those words pierced her heart, stabbing her with a guilt she couldn't rationalize.

"I miss you too, Brad," she replied shakily. "But I really must go, honey. Goodby, now. I'll call you soon."

She replaced the phone, staring at her desk for several minutes before picking up the first letter from a pile of correspondence to be answered.

The announcement became official the next afternoon. Casey Green was the new co-anchor of WJAK. The news was received with mixed reactions—surprise and pleasure among friends, envy and doubt among acquaintances. Ben had been sincere in his congratulations, but she sensed in Coy a wariness, as though he had read her own troubled thoughts.

If only I could predict *Steve's* response, she thought, a pleasurable glow filling her at the sound of his voice over the telephone.

"Casey! Congratulations!" His reaction was enthusiastic. "I knew you'd get it. You're the best."

"Thanks, Steve. Maybe I should have taken more time before accepting the offer, but it seemed like the sensible thing to do." She frowned, her voice holding a hint of uncertainty.

"Of course it was! When can we have a celebration dinner?"

She ached to see him, to open her heart to him, voicing every doubt and frustration that had troubled her during the past week. Glancing down at her scribbled calendar, however, she realized the hope was only a dream.

"I'm sorry, Steve," she hated herself for her next words, "but I don't have a spare minute. There are meetings after work and shopping to do. My entire wardrobe has to be revamped."

"Maybe some other time," he replied, the old pride adding a note of reserve to his tone.

Her lips parted, an apology forming, but the words died in her throat as she thought again of the futility of their situation.

"Yes, some other time," she echoed miserably.

Late that evening, Casey dragged herself into the kitchen, placing a bowl of soup in the microwave while sipping warm milk to soothe her nervous stomach.

The congratulatory flowers from her parents, a flood of phone calls from fans, and a wide smile on the face of Mr. Rosenthall should have combined to make her ecstatic. So why did she feel such a void in her heart? Was it true, as she had heard, that a long-awaited goal, once achieved, often perversely leaves one empty, unfulfilled?

Depends on the goal, she thought dully, as the

timer jingled and she opened the door to retrieve her hot soup. It wasn't as though she had rocketed to the status of Barbara Walters. This was merely the top rung of the local ladder—the beginning, if she was serious about pursuing her career.

She had never wanted to be a television personality, having to worry about a wardrobe of fashionable clothes, the right cosmetics, the best hair style. Just yesterday, Ben had pointed out that a female anchor must be pretty enough to win public approval, but not too pretty to detract from the news she was delivering.

Casey forced herself to drink her milk as she sat analyzing her feelings. She missed her rapport with the man on the street. Interviewing people had been her main source of enjoyment, particularly people who were an inspiration to others—like the handicapped artist who had been the object of an article she had written for a popular magazine. The woman had been immensely successful with her paintings, giving God the credit for her talent.

Reaching for one of the newspapers she read each evening in an effort to keep current with all the news, her weary eyes scanned the columns briefly, then her dark lashes fluttered, drooped, closed. The newspaper floated down from her relaxed fingers as she gave in to a deep exhausted sleep.

By the next week Casey had yielded to Steve's persistent invitations for lunch, meeting him at a restaurant near her office. Their time together had been strained, however, as neither was able to restore the light-hearted mood that had prevailed on their day in the mountains.

Finally, when Casey could no longer bear the mounting tension, she made polite excuses for a quick return to work. Steve's strong hand gripped her elbow, halting her at the door.

"I have a deep dark secret that I've never confessed," the blue eyes appraised her seriously.

"What is it?" she spun around, wide-eyed.

"I used to be a gourmet cook!" he whispered.

She stared at him for a moment, then burst into laughter. "I never would have guessed."

"And now that you know, I've decided to share my culinary talents with you, particularly since you've dropped at least five pounds in the past two weeks." The blue eyes studied her trim figure with concern.

"Is it that noticeable?" she frowned.

"I'm going to make you an offer you can't refuse. I'm taking the day off tomorrow. Why don't I go grocery shopping and have a nice meal prepared when you arrive home?"

She blinked at him, realizing he had never seen the inside of her cluttered apartment, small and dull compared to his luxurious home.

"Well, why the hesitation?" he squeezed her arm, the blue eyes insistent. "I've given you a day's notice to stash your laundry and hide the dirty dishes."

She laughed, shaking her head in resignation. "You're just too smart! You've obviously zeroed in on one of my weaknesses."

"I'm afraid I'm blind to your weaknesses," he smiled down at her. "Amazing, isn't it?"

"Yes," she echoed, the old longing gripping her heart once more.

"Well," he finally broke the spell, "how will I get in to your apartment?"

"Oh," she blinked, thinking. "I keep a key hidden under the flowerpot by my porch step. Use that one. Hey, Steve," she placed a hand on his arm, "are you sure you want to go to all this trouble just to play chef?"

"I can't think of anything I'd *rather* do!"

"Then how can I refuse?" she tiptoed up to return his good-by kiss, aware that she was the one who was blind. But for the moment, she didn't care.

CHAPTER 7

"SURPRISE!"

Steve greeted her at the door, dressed in Levis and blue, button-down shirt, a bath towel knotted thickly about his waist.

"I like your apron," Casey laughed, her eyes flicking over him appreciatively.

The weariness that had drugged her after the newscast was suddenly evaporating, replaced by a warm glow tingling through her veins, lifting her spirits as Steve leaned down to press a kiss on her cheek.

"Do come in." He stepped aside, waving her in with a broad sweep of his arm. "I've timed the meal just right. Aren't you impressed?"

"Definitely! What is that heavenly smell?" She sniffed the spicy aroma as he helped her out of her coat.

"Beef stroganoff!" he announced proudly, smiling down at her. "Used to be one of my specialties." His arm encircled her shoulder as they entered the living room, Casey unconsciously leaning against his side. "During my lean years of law school, I landed a job as an assistant cook in a very exclusive restaurant," he explained. "I never thought of myself as a chef, but I came to really enjoy my stint at cooking. When I left law school, I left the restaurant business as well. But then," he motioned her to the sofa, "when I married a woman who couldn't cook, I found myself rattling the pots and pans again. I did all the cooking during our first years of marriage." His tone was light and pleasant, with no trace of resentment.

Casey sank onto the sofa, automatically swinging her legs up to rest her feet on the coffee table. Steve leaned down, slipping the spike heels from her feet as she watched, fascinated.

"Fortunately, we could soon afford a cook and housekeeper," he grinned at her, his capable fingers gently massaging the ache from her weary feet.

"What do you think you're doing?" she stared at him, almost moaning with relief as the stiff muscles began to relax beneath his kneading fingers.

"I'm rubbing your tired feet. They *are* tired, aren't they?"

"Dead is a better word," she groaned. "I don't know if my feet always ache because I buy uncomfortable shoes, or if I'm just not supposed to walk on my feet like other mortals. Maybe I was destined to sit on a cushion and watch you cook," she quipped, the brown eyes dancing with humor.

"I wouldn't mind," he said quietly, the serious blue gaze holding her captive.

In silence they stared, the electrical awareness that had surrounded their relationship mounting as an unspoken message passed between them.

The oven timer buzzed, breaking their thoughtful mood. Steve leapt to his feet, racing toward the kitchen. "Saved by the bell," he called over his shoulder, laughing.

Casey laughed too, struggling to her feet, padding barefoot across to the china cabinet. Opening the louvered doors, she pulled down her best dinner plates, along with her crystal water goblets and gleaming silver utensils. On an impulse, she reached down into a bottom drawer and pulled out a pair of silver candelabra, and a gold linen cloth.

By the time she had set a cozy table in the small dining area, Steve had loaded the main dish and tossed salad onto a serving tray and was bringing the meal out, a shy grin on his full lips.

Casey filled the water glasses, then hurried back to the table as he lit the candles.

"Might as well do it right," he grinned at her, walking over to flick off the overhead lights. "Wait a minute," he paused, his hand on the switch, "something is missing."

Smoothing a wrinkle from the tablecloth, Casey appraised the table quickly, checking for salt, pepper, butter. . .

"Music!" he reminded her. "That *is* a stereo in the corner, isn't it?"

She laughed, shaking her head in frustration. "I told you, my brain doesn't function after working hours." She joined him at the stack of records on the shelf, and together, they chose a soothing instrumental, one of her favorites. Then he followed her to the table, pulling the chair back as she sat down, pleased by so much attention.

"Well," he paused beside her, lifting the platter of stroganoff so that she could serve herself, "I'm not making any guarantees about the food. But I hope it's passable."

"Mmmm," she breathed a sigh of pleasure, "I have no doubt it's exceptional! Please don't serve me," she

102

insisted with a small laugh. "Sit down over there and let's get started."

As he took his seat, she bowed her head, offering grace for the meal. She also gave thanks for the opportunity to share this meal with Steve, then shyly added a request that God would bless their friendship.

"That was an interesting prayer," Steve said after she had finished. "Do you really believe God bothers about such things as relationships between mortals?"

"Of course He does!"

Steve unfolded his napkin, avoiding her sincere gaze.

When she realized he was not going to say more, she commented on the food. "This is delicious!" she exclaimed. "You are an excellent cook."

He shrugged. "I was afraid I might have lost my touch. It's been a while since I've tied on an apron. But I do hope you enjoy it. I want to be certain that you get a square meal. You mustn't lose any more weight, Casey."

"After this meal, I'm sure to have gained at least a pound," she teased. "Thanks, Steve. You're very thoughtful."

"Actually my motive was more selfish than you think," he grinned. "I figured if I could bribe you with food, I could see you again. I'm beginning to realize something, though." He lowered his fork to his plate, his eyes pinning hers. "One meal isn't enough."

"Oh?" She stared at him, lips parted in surprise.

"Sitting here with you tonight, enjoying a quiet meal together, makes me aware of what I've been missing." He turned back to his food. "In case you haven't noticed, I can't seem to get by without seeing you. I need your strength, or your charm, or whatever has turned my head."

She looked away, confused. The time had come to express her doubts, she realized with a sinking heart, dreading to begin the conversation, yet knowing she must. For now, however, it could wait, she decided.

She forced herself to finish the meal, devouring every bite. Steve followed suit, interpreting her silence as a tribute to his fine food. Finally, when she couldn't hold another bite, Casey stood up.

"I think I'll put on a pot of coffee," she suggested.

"A woman after my heart," he nodded, beginning to gather up dishes, as she returned to the kitchen to spoon coffee into the percolater.

"Just leave the dishes," she called between counting spoonfuls.

"I'll do no such thing! By the way," he entered the kitchen, balancing a stack of dishes in his arms, "you didn't compliment my tidy kitchen."

She plugged the coffee in, then glanced around. "Thanks, again. I'm beginning to feel obligated, and that isn't an emotion I'm accustomed to dealing with."

"I hope you start feeling *very* obligated." His arms reached out, pulling her to him, as his lips came down on hers, testing, then settling firmly over hers. Casey found herself responding automatically, as if it were the most natural thing in the world to be resting in his arms at the end of the day.

The kiss deepened, sending a warm glow through Casey, reminding her that no man had ever affected her in quite this way. Just when her fingers twitched to slip up his shoulders and wind through his thick hair, she pulled away, shaking her head sadly.

"Steve, there's something I must say to you," she began, struggling to control her breathlessness.

"Sounds serious. Maybe we'd better sit down." He guided her back to the sofa, the soft music playing on as they sat in the semidarkness of the living room, the candles still wavering bravely on the deserted table.

Casey reached for a sofa pillow, her fingers toying

nervously with the fringe. "I realized after you confided in me about Scarlett that our relationship could never progress beyond the friendship stage." She felt the color rising in her cheeks, aware that her words might sound presumptuous.

"What do you mean?" The dark head inclined, studying her carefully.

"Don't you see? I'm just another busy version of your wife!" She turned to him, the brown eyes pained.

"You're not at all like Scarlett." Steve leaned against the sofa, the blue gaze drifting toward the ceiling, remembering.

"I'm certainly not as beautiful!" The words burst from her throat before her teeth ground into her bottom lip.

"Beauty comes from within." He reached for her hand, lifting her fingers to his lips. "You're a lovely woman, Casey, but Brad and I appreciate the inner beauty even more. Listen to me," he kissed her fingers, then held her hand firmly, covering it with both his own, "I think you misunderstood what I was saying the other day. I respected Scarlett for her talent, just as I respect you for yours, but Scarlett was totally absorbed in her work. She placed such high demands on herself that I'll always believe stress contributed to her illness." He shook his dark head as though loosening a painful memory. "Anyway, I didn't mean to indicate that Brad and I need a woman who is so devoted to us that she has no other life. I would never demand that of anyone—"

"But—" she broke off, trying to check her speeding thoughts. If she pursued this line of reasoning, she would soon be discussing her potential as a wife, and she certainly was not ready to think of that!

"Casey, is this why you've been avoiding me? I had

105

begun to think you just weren't interested, but I couldn't give up."

"No," she laughed softly, her brown eyes glowing, "and I can't imagine your giving up on anything, Steve Simpson!"

"The odd thing is," he began, his blue gaze drifting toward the flickering candles, his expression pensive, "I've been behaving totally out of character ever since I met you. Strangely, I can feel myself softening, becoming the more caring person I've always wanted to be." He turned to her, a disturbed frown rumpling his dark brows. "I can see that I've become hardened to life, maybe as a result of steeling myself to courtroom trauma, or maybe from watching someone I cared about die a slow painful death at the peak of her life. I don't know," he shrugged, "but I like myself better. If I don't watch it, I'll soon be helping little old ladies across the street and using my spare time for charitable work." The blue eyes darted across to her, glinting mischievously.

"An admirable departure from that stern-faced lawyer I first encountered!" she laughed. "But I suspect you assist little old ladies anyway, and I remember reading that you chaired an important fundraiser last year, so don't be trying to paint too black a picture of yourself." She tapped his shoulder lightly. "I know better. And besides, no other person can change you from within. Only God can do that."

He stared at her in thoughtful silence, his face solemn.

"Steve, I really wish you'd start attending church with Brad. I feel so guilty that I can't take him now," she admitted, frowning.

His eyelids closed, as he leaned back beside her, the dark wavy hair falling casually about his face as he rested his head against the sofa.

"Casey, I haven't been inside a church since Scarlett died."

"But," she swallowed, her thoughts racing, "Steve, surely you don't blame God for her death. And you must think of Brad. He needs to be in Sunday school, learning with other children." She shook her head, her eyes reflecting her troubled thoughts. "Steve, I just can't believe God is responsible for death, especially a slow painful death. Things happen that we don't understand, but," she reached across to him, her hand squeezing his, "we have to go on. Please come to church," she begged softly. "I'm not wise enough to give you the answers, but God is."

He sat up, his gaze running over her pleading face. "Maybe I'll try it again. I attended church a few times when I was young, but I gave it up. Maybe I'll try it your way for a change."

Casey looked deep into his eyes, a warm smile curving her lips. There was no need for words.

Silently he pulled her into his arms, and she returned his gentle kiss. Their passion was subdued by a sense of reverence for the new discoveries they were making together. Casey noticed the difference— and sent a happy little prayer winging heavenward.

Throughout the following week, despite her efforts to concentrate, Casey's thoughts kept drifting toward Steve, her desire to be with him increasing until she pushed her work aside and joined him for lunch on two of her busiest days. She was aware of her co-workers regarding her with puzzled expressions, yet everyone remained tactfully silent.

Everyone, that is, except Coy.

"What is it with you?" He leaned down over her desk one morning when she was feeling exceptionally happy. "You go around grinning like a Cheshire cat,

107

and there's a look in those big brown eyes that definitely has not been there before!''

Casey looked up from her work, smiling dreamily. ''Coy, I think I'm falling in love,'' she admitted.

He nodded, one broad hand stroking his beard. ''That's what I was afraid of!''

''What do you mean *afraid of*?'' she bristled, leaning closer. ''Steve Simpson is a wonderful man!''

Coy flinched, batting his pale lids in frustration. ''That's even worse. Steve Simpson! Casey, the man is cold and ruthless.'' He shook his shaggy head in obvious amazement that she could fall for the shrewd attorney.

''You're wrong, Coy. He may *appear* that way, but people change. Steve has,'' she replied softly.

Coy groaned. ''I hate to see you get stepped on the first time out, kid. It *is* the first time, isn't it?''

Casey crossed her arms and fixed a bright determined gaze on the big man. ''Which proves my judgment is more sound than you think. Your problem, Coy, is that you have no faith in human nature. In fact, you have no faith, *period*,'' she added gently, ''which is another part of your problem.''

Coy glared at her for a tense moment, then glanced self-consciously around the newsroom. ''Hey, Green, I've missed you. I admit it!'' He turned back to her. ''You have a way of setting me straight like no one else. Except maybe Sharon.'' His big jaw dropped, pain settling over his face in a tragic mask.

''Coy, why don't you two get back together?'' Casey asked earnestly. ''I know you still love her— and she loves you! I was talking to her last week when she came by to leave some mail for you. *She still loves you*, Coy.''

''I'm so lonely without her and the children,'' Coy sighed, shifting his weight. But I just can't believe she'd ever forgive me for the mess I made of our

108

marriage. Once you start lying and deceiving, Casey, well—it just wouldn't work."

Casey stared at him for a moment, then reached under her desk, dragging out her bulging tote bag. Plunging into its depths, she pulled out her worn New Testament and handed it to him. "Read this, Coy," she insisted. "The answers to all your problems are in this Book."

He hesitated, glancing nervously around the room.

"Take it." She pushed the Bible into his hand, breathing a sigh of relief when he accepted it awkwardly, then turned and bounded out of the newsroom.

"I actually enjoyed the church service," Steve admitted, taking Casey's arm as they walked back to the car. Brad lingered behind, hurling a rock into the distance.

"I'm glad," Casey smiled, turning to wave to friends as Steve unlocked the door of his Continental and she stood waiting, recalling the admiring glances cast in their direction during the service.

At lunch, as they were ushered to a table at one of Colorado Springs' posh resort hotels, Casey was again aware of appreciative glances and murmured comments: ". . . the new co-anchor on Channel Six . . ." ". . . even prettier in real life . . ."

Casey was often recognized in public places. Being on display did not bother her, nor did it affect her in the same way it did others who enjoyed their celebrity status. She merely thought of herself as a working girl who was conscientious about her job. If she felt an added measure of importance today, it was because she was sharing a Sunday with two people who seemed to need her.

The mood was relaxed as they studied the oversized menus.

"How did you happen to get a Sunday off?" Steve inquired after chuckling over Brad's order—a hamburger and french fries in this five-star restaurant!

"By putting my foot down," she sighed, recalling uncomfortably the degree of assertiveness it had taken to make her point. "Not only that—but I'm going to start taking an occasional day off. I have sick leave and vacation time coming."

"Really?" Steve's dark brows arched with interest. "For starters, then, how about next weekend? That would give the three of us two whole days for a short vacation in Vail."

"Vail!" whooped Brad. "You mean we can all go? That's super, since I didn't get to go last time—" he broke off, the reminder of those days creating sudden tension.

"I think a weekend in Vail sounds like a marvelous idea," Casey interjected, smoothing the awkward moment. "Would you believe that I've lived in Colorado all this time, and I've never yet seen Vail?"

The happy expressions on the faces of the two men in her life buoyed Case for the rest of the week."

CHAPTER 8

The wheels of Steve's jeep crunched over the snow-plowed streets of Vail, approaching the cream and brown condominiums from a back street designated for autos. Further down in the village, the streets were zoned for pedestrians, with skiers in colorful attire wandering idly among the shops and boutiques, unhampered by traffic.

"What a storybook setting," Casey sighed, her gaze lifting from the European-style town to the white ski slopes dotted with tiny figures designing swoops and arcs with deceptive ease.

"Vail is the largest ski complex in North America," Steve informed her, "with about ten square miles of skiing terrain."

"Amazing," Casey murmured, glancing up at the brown balconies of the condominiums where neat little rows of firewood were carefully stacked.

The sight of the firewood brought her attention back to the snow still mounded on parked cars, lampposts, and rooftops, despite the dazzling morning sun.

Steve turned into the parking space and cut the engine. Casey glanced into the back seat at Brad's still form, huddled into the sleeping bag. "I can't believe he slept all the way," she mused.

"Brad has never been an early riser, particularly on Saturdays. And his passion for sleeping late was one of the reasons I suggested we get an early start. I figured if I could drag him out of bed and load him into the jeep, he would sleep through the trip, giving us an opportunity to enjoy the scenery—without interruption." He winked mischievously.

"I see," Casey grinned. "Well, do we have very much to unload?"

"*We* don't. I'll let you carry in your overnighter, but Brad and I can manage the rest."

Casey glanced toward the luggage area, aware that Steve's skiis were obviously missing.

"Steve, I still feel badly that you didn't plan to do any skiing simply because I'm too cowardly to tackle the slopes."

"Listen—" the blue eyes gleamed darkly above the white, cable-knit sweater, "I've been coming up here for years, but this is the first time I've had the privilege of bringing *you*. Besides, I'd rather introduce you to Vail. It's such a unique little place."

"And I want to see it," she nodded, pushing the car door open and hopping out.

"Brad, we're here, buddy." Steve was prodding his son awake in the back seat while Casey zipped her bright red parka and stretched up on the toes of her thick-soled hiking boots. Her crisp Levis dragged against her skin, stiff and new.

Glancing back at Steve in his faded Levis and soft ski sweater, she wished that she'd had the good sense to wear her favorite jeans, rather than rushing out to buy a new pair that were still short of perfect comfort by a few washings.

Brad, also, had worn practical clothing. In fact, his little jeans had faded beyond respectability and his thick ski sweater had seen plenty of action as well.

An appreciative smile touched her lips as she gazed at Brad, admiring the thick mop of dark hair tumbling over his sleepy face. The trip had meant so much to him! She had prayed all week long that nothing would happen to prevent their coming.

Steve was hooking a lightweight bag over Brad's arm, along with Casey's make-up case, then he hoisted a garment bag and suitcase and turned back to lock the car.

Casey reached down and lifted her overnighter, bearing three changes of clothes for her short stay, evidence of her excitement and inability to decide on which outfits to pack.

"Watch your step!" Steve called over his shoulder as he led the way up the circular steps to the second story of the large building.

At the second landing, Casey paused, glancing down below to Vail Village, where quaint little shops and restaurants reminded her of a picture she had once seen of a Bavarian town.

"Dad, do you think the Andersons will be here this weekend?" Brad asked, yawning.

"Well, I saw their station wagon down in the parking lot." Steve glanced at the parked cards. "The Andersons are our neighbors," he explained to Casey. "They have a son who is a couple of years older than Brad."

The door creaked as Steve turned the key in the lock and pushed the door wide. Casey's glance swept the cozy living room, decorated in green and blue plaids, with moss green carpeting.

"You can have my room, Casey," Brad offered. "I'm gonna sleep with Dad."

"That's very nice of you, Brad." She glanced down

113

the hallway that separated two bedrooms and led to an adjoining bath.

"It's the room on the right there, if you want to hang up your clothes." Steve nodded toward the room, turning sideways to negotiate the load down the narrow hall.

Casey followed, glancing at the bedroom on the left, a master bedroom, then turning into a cozy little room, perfectly decorated for Brad. Pictures of skiers and athletes covered the pine-paneled walls. The bedspread and matching draperies were designed with football pennants, adding a splash of color to the room. She placed her bag beside the small closet, then turned to glance at her reflection in the little dresser mirror.

Her hair was mussed and her lip gloss had disappeared, but her brown eyes were glowing and her cheeks looked rosy from the invigorating cold. Strange how love could alter the appearance, she thought with amusement, as she unzipped her coat and laid it across the bed.

At the sound of strange voices, she pushed her door closed, dragging a brush through her hair, then plunging in her purse for her make-up kit. Soon there was a tap on the door, and she opened it to a smug-looking Steve.

"That was Bill Anderson and his son Chuck. They saw us arriving. Chuck has invited Brad to have lunch with them and walk over to the slopes. Naturally, I agreed." His mouth quirked in a conspiratorial grin.

"Well, it's nice that Brad has a friend here," she replied.

"What's *really* nice is that Chuck is a couple of years older than Brad and is the tolerant type. Come on," he reached for her hand, "I want to show you something."

Her brows lifted in anticipation as she followed him back to the living room.

"Vail has given you a very special welcome," he called over his shoulder, as he led her to the sliding glass door, turning the latch and opening it wide.

Tiny little snowflakes whirled through the air, bringing a gasp of surprise from Casey.

"But the sun was shining when we got here!" she shook her head, fascinated. "Of course, I should have learned by now that Colorado weather is subject to change without notice. Oh, Steve," her face was alight, "could we go for a walk in the snow? This is too lovely to miss."

"Sure we can." He gave her an indulgent smile and helped her bundle into her warm outerwear.

As they hurried out the door and down the steps, Casey lifted wondering eyes to the swirling snowflakes, marveling at their softness as they feathered over her face.

"Isn't it funny?" she said. "In Colorado Springs I'd be complaining about shoveling the stuff or getting to work on time. But here the snow merely adds to the magic."

"Yeah, I know," Steve looked up at the swollen gray clouds.

"It's like talcum powder," she laughed, impulsively sticking out her tongue to catch a flake.

"That's why Vail is such a popular resort," Steve grinned at her. "The best skiing is done in this kind of powder. The skis move over it with little resistance, yet there's enough body to the packed snow to support a skier."

"I still wish you had brought your skis." She looked at him with regret.

"I'd rather spend my time with you. Maybe the next time we come, I'll bring them."

"The next time?" she echoed, silently admiring his dark profile against the stark white wonderland.

"The next time," he repeated, the rich blue gaze challenging her to offer resistance. But then why would she want to? she wondered, her heart singing.

She had opened her mouth to agree when a group of college kids jostled against her, bringing her head around in surprise. The attractive young men and women were dressed in jeans, insulated vests, and flannel shirts, their sun-bronzed faces evidence of their days on the slopes. Laughing and carefree, they were scarcely aware that their crowd had taken up the entire sidewalk.

"Everyone has a good time here." Steve studied the group with a tolerant grin. "In fact, a good time always prevails. You just automatically take a deep breath and slow down."

He guided Casey into a small coffee shop, the gold-lettered plate glass windows advertising hot drinks and homemade sweet rolls.

"Are you hungry?" he asked, opening the door for her.

"I hadn't thought about it lately," she laughed as they entered the sweet shop where the aroma of freshly baked bread, rich coffee, and herbed teas set her taste buds tingling.

She hadn't dared confess to Steve that she'd skipped breakfast when he picked her up at eight this morning. Now, sharpened by their stroll through the snow, her appetite asserted itself and she discovered that she was ravenously hungry.

They chose a booth near the window so that they could look out on the distant mountain range, blanketed with fresh snow.

"Tell me about Vail," she looked across at Steve. "I can't believe I haven't been here before, and I'm afraid I'm your typical tourist at heart," she shrugged, grinning.

"Then where's your camera?"

"I forgot it," she moaned, regretting that she hadn't set the alarm clock an hour earlier.

"Well, you asked for it," he teased. "This valley was once the summer home of the Ute Indians. Later a British nobleman named Lord Gore started a settlement here. That was around 1880, I think. There's a creek and a mountain range named after him. But the fantastic ski potential wasn't realized until some World War II paratroopers did their training here. After the war, they returned and started the skiing industry."

He paused, sipping his coffee. "This is my favorite vacation spot in all the world—summer as well as winter. Of course, I love to ski, but you can come up in the summer for horseback riding, or just to enjoy the good food and relaxing atmosphere. The locals have provided a lot of interesting things to attract people year round now."

When the coffee and sweet rolls were served, Casey did not hesitate to grab a bite of the gooey roll. "Why are you looking at me like that?" she asked, licking cinnamon sugar from her fingers.

"I'm thinking how much I enjoy watching *you* enjoy yourself."

She licked her lips, then sipped the coffee. "And are *you* enjoying yourself?" she asked.

"As I told you, Casey, I need you," he replied simply.

She smiled at him, her brown eyes glowing. "And I need you," she said softly, thinking how drastically her life had changed since they met.

After they had finished their coffee and were walking back through the snow, Casey was aware of a sensation of deep contentment. She had never known it was possible to experience this kind of happiness with another human being.

In the beginning their relationship had been tense and strained, and yet there had been an electrical awareness between them. Now, though the electricity had receded to the background, surfacing at poignant moments, they had progressed to another level, a quiet deep appreciation of one another and an obsession to spend every moment together.

Casey glanced up at Steve as they neared the condominium. Would this last? Could it? She looked away, frightened by the sudden intensity of her feelings. And how would she handle the heartbreak if she should lose him?

She shook her head, falling silent, the sound of their booted heels crunching into the snow the only accompaniment to their thoughts.

Brad and Chuck were in the parking lot throwing snowballs when Casey and Steve arrived. Chuck, a tall blond boy whose wide smile and easy-going temperment won Casey's instant approval, asked if he and Brad could walk over to the slopes to observe the beginners.

Steve agreed, shoving a bill into Brad's hand for hot chocolate later. Then he and Casey climbed the stairs to the condominium, the high altitude making them pant for breath.

Once inside, before they had removed their coats, Steve caught her to him, lowering his lips to her warm mouth. Casey responded, lifting her arms to his neck, relishing the cold sweet taste of him. As their kiss deepened, the blood pounded through her veins, bringing a sudden inexplicable fear. She pulled away, wide-eyed.

"What's wrong?" he asked, startled.

She swallowed, staring down at her clenched hands. "I'm frightened," she admitted softly.

118

His arms slid around her shoulders, pulling her back against his chest. "Don't be frightened," he said huskily. "Your feelings are perfectly normal, perfectly adult. Ah, Casey," he sighed, "I keep forgetting that the renowned television lady is still a shy little girl at heart."

"Don't make fun," her voice trembled. "I can't help it if I've never been in love before." She bit her lip, closing her eyes against her sudden blunder.

"Are you serious?" he asked, pressing a kiss into the warm softness of her neck. "About being in love, I mean?"

She wandered over and sat down on the sofa, averting her gaze from his, as she struggled with words.

"Would you like to take off your coat?" he asked softly.

"Oh, yes! It is a little warm, isn't it?" A sheepish smile curved her lips. She shrugged out of her jacket and handed it to him, leaning back on the sofa to take a deep strengthening breath as he went to hang their wraps in the closet.

Her eyes lifted slowly to meet his intent blue gaze as he sat down on the sofa beside her, reaching for her hand.

"Hey, don't be embarrassed," he said. "I've been acting like a teen-ager ever since I met you, spouting off angry words one minute, then melting at your feet the next. It's awkward for a thirty-six-year-old man to talk about falling head-over-heels in love. But I *am* in love with you!"

Her eyes widened, new happiness filling their depths.

"I'm also having trouble keeping my hands off you, as you've no doubt noticed." A wry grin touched his lips.

"And I'm having strong feelings when you hold me

and kiss me," she paused, wondering how to voice her scruples without sounding like a prude.

"So?" he prompted, watching her carefully.

"I know this is the twentieth century and people seem to be caught up in a sexual revolution, but I'm not one of them. As I just told you, I've never fallen in love before, and I'm awed by it." Her voice trembled, as she studied his serious face, wondering what he was thinking.

"Listen to me," he said finally. "I'm looking for something far more lasting than a one-night stand or a quick fling. I tried to run from you in the beginning. I hid behind my anger and my silly threats until I realized you were too kind and forgiving to hold a grudge."

His long fingers traced a circle over the back of her hand, as his deep blue gaze slipped over her head to the glass window, studying the snow thickening in the soft white world beyond their door.

"Casey," he turned back, his face solemn, "would you consider marrying me?"

"You want me to—marry you?" she gasped. She had considered the idea, of course, but had always stopped short—fully aware of the serious obstacles between them.

"I . . . don't know, Steve," she shook her head, confused.

"You just said you were in love with me," he reminded her, his dark brows lifted quizzically.

"I am," she nodded, "but we aren't ready for marriage yet. There are other factors to consider."

"Such as?"

"My job."

"We can work that out."

"Your lack of commitment to my faith," she continued, the pain of her words bringing a lump to her throat. "A person's religious beliefs are very important in choosing a marriage partner."

Steve pulled away, his gaze drifting around the room, his face clouded with doubt. "That's something I can't share, Casey. Not yet. Honey, you're so determined, so committed to everything you do. And your faith," he paused, seeking the right word, "is just about as strong as that snow-capped mountain out there. But that's not for me. I've grown too cynical."

Casey stared at him, considering his words. She loved Steve as she had never loved another man. And she was willing to love Brad as though he were her own. But neither she nor Steve was ready for a commitment, she realized, as his lean features hardened in thought, the dark brows slashed in contemplation.

"I don't think you're cynical, Steve." She touched his arm lightly. "But we do need more time. Perhaps time will solve everything—"

"Time and togetherness," he confirmed, a relieved smile softening the lines around his mouth. "But at least—" The hard thumping on the door signaled the boys' return, and Steve stood up, crossing the room. "At least we've admitted our true feelings. That's a start." He winked across at her before opening the door to receive a miniature snowman—Brad, covered from head to foot with the powdery white stuff.

They spent the afternoon browsing through the shops and boutiques in the village, then dining at a popular local restaurant where an elegant meal was served by candlelight. Afterwards the three of them trudged back through the snow to the condominium, their arms linked.

"I've had a good time today," Brad yawned. "Haven't you guys?"

"A very good time," Casey nodded, staring up through the snowy night to the twinkling lights of Vail, and beyond them, to the vast starry expanse above.

"A great time," Steve squeezed her arm. "And this is just the beginning."

CHAPTER 9

THE PRESSURE OF a hectic Monday morning failed to
dampen Casey's exuberant spirits as she raced
through her work, her heart singing with joy. Steve
was scarcely out of her mind for more than a few
minutes, before a word, a song, an idea, sent her
thoughts hurtling back to him.

They met for lunch on Monday and Tuesday, each
drawing strength from the other as they related their
breathless schedules.

By Wednesday, however, Casey's happy mood was
challenged.

"Look at this!" She waved a news report at Mr.
Rosenthall who was sauntering by her desk. "There's
a terrific story here, but we're only touching the
surface!"

He reached for the report, scanning its contents.
"A high school student saves a woman from her
burning home. So?"

She stared at him, her mouth dropping open. "I
wouldn't consider that an everyday occurrence,

would you? Look at that last line," she pointed.
"When the reporter asked him how it felt to be a hero,
he said he just did what anyone else would have done.
Don't you think that's remarkable coming from a
sixteen-year-old who was running late for school?"

Mr. Rosenthall shrugged a shoulder of his Brooks
Brothers suit, then handed the report back to her, his
thin face passive. "Yes, quite remarkable." He
turned to go.

"But Mr. Rosenthall," she sputtered, glaring after
him, "why doesn't someone interview this boy for a
special?" She glanced over the report again. "He
risked his life. I think he deserves more recognition
than his name and age, don't you?"

Mr. Rosenthall glanced back over his shoulder.
"I'll tell Ben. In the meantime, Miss Green, I think
you should remember that you're now an anchor, not
an on-the-street reporter."

Anger surged within, flaming her cheeks and leaving her mouth dry. She slumped in her chair, staring
down at the pages trembling in her hands.

"Cool it," Mona warned under her breath as she
darted by the desk, her face revealing stunned
disbelief.

"I don't feel like cooling it!" Casey whirled on her.
"When there's some senseless murder, we give the
bad guy prime time. When a young boy risks his life,
we dismiss it with some flippant good-for-you remark
and crowd the story into forty-five seconds. I don't
like that, Mona!" her voice rose indignantly.

"Will you settle down?" Ben's sharp words spun
her around, and she was looking straight into his icy
stare. "You'd better control your tongue, little lady,"
he warned before spinning on his heel and taking off.

"I—" Casey clamped her lips together, struggling
to regain control. What had gotten into her? How

could she possibly have presumed to tell Mr. Rosenthall what to do? Even Ben would never do that.

Nervously she flipped through the typewritten pages on her desk, trying to analyze her bad behaviour. She missed her interviews, that was it! She missed the opportunity to pursue a Christian approach to news reporting.

She bit her lip, trying to concentrate on the report before her as the telephone rang, breaking into her thoughts.

"Casey Green," she breathed into the receiver, wondering what the next crisis would bring.

"Hello, Casey Green," Steve's voice filled the wire. "How's my favorite anchor?"

"Not so good," she mumbled into the receiver. "My temper just got the best of me again, Steve."

"Wish I could come over and calm you down," he replied soothingly. "But I'm calling to let you know that Brad and I are going up to Denver for a couple of days to visit my sister Jane. He has a school holiday and she has been pestering us to come. Wish you could join us," he added softly.

She swallowed around the aggravating lump in her throat. The idea of walking out of her tension-charged office for a couple of carefree days with Steve and Brad was so tempting that, for a moment, she feared she would burst into childish tears.

"I wish I could see you, but Brad and I are running late. I just wanted you to know that I'll miss you!" He paused, waiting. "Aren't you going to reply to that last statement?"

"I'll miss you, too," she sighed. "More than you know."

"Ah, just what I wanted to hear! Listen, I'll call you as soon as I get back in town, and we'll have dinner together. Be sure to save some time for me!"

"I will," she said, wishing she didn't feel so despondent. "Have a safe trip—and a good time."

"I would have a *better* time if you were going. Have a good week, honey. And remember—I love you!"

She closed her eyes, savoring the special lift that his words gave her. "Thanks, Steve," she murmured. "I love you, too."

When she had lowered the phone to its cradle, she leaned back in her chair, tapping her pencil against the desk. Through the far window, she noticed Pikes Peak, sprawling across the western horizon.

Her thoughts drifted back to the special time in Vail, when she and Steve had opened their hearts and confessed their feelings.

"Your faith is as strong as that mountain," Steve had said, his eyes filling with love.

The memory of their conversation made her consider his proposal again. Should she insist on their waiting to get married? Did she really want to wait? Of course she didn't! But she had to be sensible for both of them, and for Brad as well. For as Steve had admitted, in matters of the heart his cool logic fled.

Her desk phone pealed out again—this time with a request for a staff conference. She sighed, pushing her chair back from the desk and rising wearily to her feet.

This job is beginning to bug me, she thought, squaring her shoulders and marching off to the conference room.

Snowflakes danced down from the night skies, piling up like cake frosting on the rooftops, mounding on the limbs of cottonwoods and pines along the boulevard. The Christmas card setting added an aura of romance to the evening as Casey screeched into Steve's drive and ran up the walk to his front door.

126

Before she could lift the brass knocker, the door swung wide, and Steve was pulling her into his arms.

"I've missed you," he sighed, burying his face into the fragrant silk of her hair.

"I've missed you, too," Casey murmured against his sweatered chest, her arms slipping up his broad shoulders. He pulled her closer, pressing warm kisses on her mouth.

"What am I doing?" He pulled away, shaking his dark head. "We're standing here in the middle of the door in freezing temperature, putting on a show for the whole neighborhood! Come on in." He squeezed her hand, drawing her into the warmth of the house, where she stood trembling—more from the intensity of her emotions than from the cold.

"Here, let me take your coat." He helped her out of the heavy parka which had provided scant protection from the frigid air. "Looks like winter is finally upon us, and there's more snow in the forecast."

"I'm counting on you for a warm fire in there tonight." She nodded toward the study, flicking the flakes of snow from her slacks.

"Just so happens I have built a roaring fire in the den." His arm encircled her shoulder as they strolled down the hall. "I finally got that fireplace cleaned out, and I've even spread the bear-skin rug," he joked, looking down at her. "Hungry?"

"I'm starving," she admitted. "I missed lunch completely."

He clucked disapprovingly. "What am I going to do with you? You have no regard for your health. Oh well, that only makes you need me more, and I just happen to have a delicious casserole in the oven."

She looked up at him. "Showing off your culinary skills again?"

"Afraid there hasn't been time. Martha fixed it up

before she and Brad left for the weekend. Come on."
His steps quickened as he pulled her into the kitchen.

"I'm glad we're eating in here." The atmosphere of
the homey red-and-white kitchen was like a hug. "For
some reason, that formal dining room makes me
jumpy."

"Really?" A dark brow arched. "Scarlett always—"
he broke off. "I'm sorry."

"Steve—" Casey's hand pressed his. "Don't apologize. I know that she was an important part of your
life. Please don't think I expect you to avoid using her
name."

"But the past is over, and with you I've found a
whole new life. . . ."

His black head bent toward her bright one, his lips
claiming hers once more in a tender, welcoming kiss.
When he pulled away and looked deep into her misty
brown eyes, he shook his head, confused.

"If I don't quit acting like a guy on his first date,
you're never going to get any dinner!"

She laughed, following Steve to the stove to inhale
the spicy aroma of the chicken casserole as he lifted it
from the oven, and cast an appreciative glance at the
freshly perked coffee. Her gaze flicked back to the
table, already set, as Steve motioned her toward a
chair.

"Perfect timing, right?" he winked at her.

"Right. Can't I pour the coffee or do something
useful?" she asked, a contented sigh slipping from her
parted lips.

"Just go sit down and look pretty. I'm developing
this protective instinct toward you that makes me feel
compelled to wait on you when you're tired. *Sit!*" He
gave a mock frown.

"You're really spoiling me, you know." She sauntered over to the table while admiring the attractive
place settings Martha had set for them.

"Good!" He placed the steaming casserole on a mat in the center of the table. "Maybe you'll decide you can't live without me!"

"Maybe I already have—"

The words slipped from her throat before she could stop them, her innate honesty making pretense impossible. He turned to her, the blue gaze darkening in obvious desire as his arms reached out, pulling her quickly to him. His lips claimed hers, more forcefully than ever.

"The coffee—" she broke away, her brown eyes glowing.

With a groan of protest, he released her, wagging his head in disapproval. "What did I do to deserve such a moral woman?" He turned back for the coffee as she seated herself at the table.

"And such a hungry one," she added, sniffing the casserole.

"Well," Steve returned with the coffee and sat down, "do we need anything else?"

"A prayer of thanks."

He nodded, shifting self-consciously in his chair. "You do the honors," he mumbled.

She offered a prayer of thanks for the food, adding a simple request that God would work in their lives, removing any obstacles that would prevent their being together, and resolving their problems.

When she whispered "Amen" and reached for the casserole, she was conscious of Steve's eyes on her, regarding her thoughtfully.

"Martha was a dear to do this," Casey said, attempting to restore their light-hearted mood. "She must have known that a certain irresponsible television reporter would be cold and hungry and had forgotten to rush to the market before it closed."

Steve laughed, taking a bite of the tasty dish, his expression registering supreme approval. Neither of

129

them spoke as they worked their way through the delicious meal, then leaned back in their chairs and relaxed.

"Want to take our coffee to the den and enjoy the fire?" he asked.

"First, we're doing the dishes," Casey insisted, rising from her chair to lift their empty plates.

"If you feel domestic, I won't argue. In fact, I should encourage it." He followed her to the sink, putting the left-overs away while she rinsed the dishes and loaded the dishwasher. "You look very much at home in this kitchen," he called from the refrigerator.

"I really like this room." Casey's gaze swung over the gleaming white cabinets and red-and-white checked wallpaper.

"But you don't like the dining room." He stood beside her, staring down with a grin.

"I don't like the dining room," she admitted softly. "I'm sorry."

He chuckled, amused by her directness.

"Then when we're married, you can redecorate the dining room. Better yet, you can redecorate the entire house! How does that sound?" He asked, refilling the coffee cups before guiding her back toward the den.

"Sounds too good to be true. That's why I don't want to rush into anything," she added thoughtfully.

"You know, Casey, rushing might be the only way I will ever get married again. I've always been so, well, sensible and pragmatic—very much the no-nonsense attorney. But when it comes to love, I lose all common sense." He opened the door into the den. "Maybe you'd better grab me now before I think twice about it," he quipped, leading her to the overstuffed sofa drawn up before a roaring fire.

She considered his words, realizing there was some truth to what he said. "Funny, isn't it?" she replied finally, watching the bright flames leap above the logs.

"I've never thought of myself as pragmatic. Sometimes I'm not even sensible. And yet, when it comes to marriage, I seem to be *very* cautious, *very* conservative."

"You must be, since you've escaped this long." He sat down beside her, his arm around the back of the sofa. "Casey, haven't you ever been in love?"

"I had a deep infatuation in college," she admitted with a shrug, "but it wore off. I guess—" she hesitated, searching for the words to express her feelings.

"Go on. You can tell me anything." The adoration in his eyes confirmed his words.

"Well, when I was a young girl, my mother told me I should start praying for the right man to share my life. It seemed silly to be uttering such a prayer when I was also asking for a date for the prom and an end to wearing braces, but I did what she suggested, if somewhat inconsistently." She studied the fire thoughtfully. "Somehow I've always had this calm assurance that my prayer would be answered. And I've known, too, that I would need enough time to learn patience and understanding in order to be a good wife and mother. It *did* take years to find you—I'll soon be twenty-five."

A look of bewildered fascination filled Steve's blue eyes as he shook his head slowly. "I don't know what I ever did to deserve a woman like you! *If* I've won you, that is." He reached for her hand. "Look, Casey, I know I have a long way to go to measure up to your standards, but if you'll just exercise some of this patience you speak of, I'll try to be everything you want in a man."

"Steve—" She pressed her fingers to his lips to silence his words. "Be what *God* wants you to be. Ultimately you must please yourself—and Him. You

131

drive yourself so hard in your work. You need to slow down and relax, enjoy your son, and—"

He pulled her fingers from his lips to voice his reply. "*And* be a deacon in the church, warm a bench on Sunday and Wednesday nights, perhaps even sing in the choir?" He groaned at the thought.

"Silly! No," she laughed softly, "those were not my requirements when I mentioned faith. The depth of your commitment is up to you. I just feel that you need to sort out some things for yourself. And so do I. Just this week I've come to a decision."

"What decision?" He pulled her against his chest, pressing kisses on her forehead, her eyelids, her cheeks.

She swallowed, trying to finish the sentence despite the warm glow his kisses brought.

"If we marry, I'm going to resign as anchor," she said, snuggling against his shoulder.

She had expected an enthusiastic reply, yet he sat very still, scarcely breathing for several seconds. His hand touched her chin, tilting her head back so that he could look into her eyes.

"Honey, I don't think that's a good idea," he said, the dark brows knitted.

"Why not?" she asked, eyes wide with surprise.

"I think you'd regret that decision later. You'd feel you had made a great sacrifice in order to be a homebody. You might even end up resenting Brad and me, whether you wanted to or not."

"I hadn't thought of it as a sacrifice," she shook her head. "You see, Steve, I have this stubborn determination that makes me tackle everything headlong. That's why I've worked so hard to be a good reporter, and now an anchor. I go over and over a story, looking for a better approach to the news. I really wouldn't have to spend as much time at my job as I do," she paused, considering. "Not every anchor puts in that many hours. It's just that when I commit myself to something, well . . . I'm committed! That's why I don't feel I could balance wife and mother with career. I know many women do that very successfully, but I don't feel that *I* could." She shook her head again. "Besides, Brad is going to need a lot of special love and care."

Steve stood up, his hand pressed to the back of his neck, long fingers massaging the nerve center there. Thoughtfully he paced the floor, his head bent. Then he stopped, turning back to her, the blue eyes burdened.

"I can't let you quit because of us, Casey."

She stared at him, trying to understand his thinking.

"It bothers me that you feel you can't balance the two. Martha is perfectly capable of taking care of the house, preparing meals, and—"

"But I *want* to help do those things," she interrupted, her eyes pleading for understanding. "Don't you see? I want to be here when Brad comes home from school. I want to try out some of my crazy recipes on you, and," she lifted her hand in an attempt to explain, "I want to do all the other housewifey things. I won't intrude on Martha's territory," she added quickly. "We'll work together, that's all."

He stood, legs braced, hands on hips, staring down at her with deeply troubled eyes.

"I've had this same argument before." He looked away from her stricken gaze. "Scarlett won out, quitting her job to, quote, 'putter around the house.' She was absolutely miserable. Seeing her in that state made me—"

"I'm not Scarlett!" Casey cried, leaping from the sofa. "And I refuse to be compared to her—it isn't fair! Surely you don't intend to hold me responsible for something she did or didn't do!" Her brown gaze begged for reassurance, her small body trembled to be held, soothed, but Steve merely stared at her, his eyes glazed and distant.

She turned for the door, unable to think beyond getting out of the room before they both said things they would later regret.

But Steve bounded across the room, his hand reaching out to restrain her, his lips quirked in a bitter grin. "No, you're not Scarlett. Listen to me, Casey. I've known you for several weeks; I was married to her for several years. And already I love you more than I ever loved her! Don't you understand how guilty that makes me feel?"

"Guilty?" she echoed, staring at him. "But, Steve, you—you can't help loving someone. You don't have to make comparisons. Just accept your feelings and stop being so paranoid about them."

"Paranoid?" he shouted, the dark brows arching. "Next, you'll be suggesting that *I* see a psychiatrist! Well, maybe you'd better examine *your* feelings. You're the one who's overreacting to my reference to Scarlett."

"Overreacting?" she gasped, the harshness in his voice a slap across her stunned face. "No, Steve, I'm reacting as any normal woman would who wants to be loved and accepted for the person she is. But if you haven't enough faith in me, and in our relationship, then you aren't ready for marriage," she said bitterly, yanking free of his grip. "Don't bother seeing me out." she jerked the door open and ran up the hall, seizing her parka from the coat rack, painfully aware that no steps advanced after her to stop her.

It was only after she had jumped into the car and sped to the next block that she allowed herself to pull over in front of a darkened house, cut the engine and give way to the choking sobs that racked her body. She felt as if an invisible knife were twisting its way through her heart, and she gasped at the sharp pain that filled her.

She had been so sure that Steve loved her, that he was willing to build a new life with her. But he kept going back to the past, punishing her, himself, for things neither of them could change.

She had tried to be patient with him, assuring him the past was over, that it was time to step into the future. What she couldn't bear was his guilt, his doubt, his lack of faith.

She lifted her tear-stained face to the web of streetlamps along the quiet boulevard, staring dismally into the haloes of light. "Maybe it's hopeless after all," she said, her throat constricting on the words. "Maybe he has scars that no one can heal."

God can heal any scar, she remembered, but Steve was unwilling to make a commitment to any sort of faith, trying to work out his life in his own way, in his own strength.

She stared at her hands trembling in her lap, suddenly aware that the cold night had penetrated the car. She shouldn't be sitting here like this. She should go home, drink a cup of hot tea, and crawl into the warm comfort of her bed.

But, perversely, she didn't want to be warm and comfortable; she wanted to wallow in her grief! Wiping the tears from her face, she took a deep breath of the piercing cold. She had to get hold of herself, she realized, trying to gain some measure of comfort from the belief that if things were meant to work out for her and Steve, they would. If not—well, she would just climb that mountain when she came to it.

She cranked the engine of her car, refusing to think further. Flicking on the headlights, she pulled away from the curb, her small body trembling from head to toe. Tossing her matted hair back from her face, she tried to force her thoughts toward her work day tomorrow, but her stubborn mind refused to budge.

Steve, I love you—I love you—

But love wasn't enough, there had to be a willingness to compromise on both sides. *Maybe neither of us is able to change*, she thought, her heart sinking again. *Maybe we're too set in our ways.*

She gripped the wheel, blinking against the tears that burned at the back of her eyes. She had heard of people who loved each other, yet were unable to reconcile their differences. Wasn't that the common complaint in divorce courts?

Well, their differences must be reconciled before she would see him again, she decided stubbornly. There was no point in going on with a man whose decisions were based on fear and doubt and guilt. And yet—

A sob erupted from her throat. *And yet I love him.* The weak little cry filled her heart again, making her aware of how vulnerable she had become. *I love him*, she thought miserably.

CHAPTER 10

"YOU HAD A FUSS with Dad, didn't you?" Brad's sharp accusation pulled Casey's mind from her busy work as she sat gripping the phone, wondering how to answer. "He's been moping around," Brad continued, gaining volume with each word. "I asked when you were coming over, and he said you *weren't*. Why aren't you?" his voice softened, his disappointment obvious.

Casey swallowed, propping an elbow on her desk as she rested her chin in the palm of her hand.

"Brad, we had a difference of opinion," she managed finally. "Neither of us could compromise. And I guess I got angry."

"Why'd you get angry?" he demanded. "What were you two fighting about?"

"Really, Brad," she shook her head wearily, "I don't have the time to go into it now. I *am* at work. Why don't you discuss this with your dad?"

"You won't tell me! You're not fair." His voice broke before he added spitefully, "*I hate you!*"

137

The bitter little cry brought her upright, her face turning white from the force of his words.

"Listen to me, Brad," she said finally. "I won't allow that kind of talk from you. Maybe you're accustomed to lashing out at people when you don't get your way, but it won't work with me. You've got to learn that you can't react with anger just to get your way!"

"I didn't get angry first," he argued back. "You did! You got mad at my dad!"

"That's right, I did," she replied, sick at heart. "But you and your dad are going to have to accept me the way I am—which means, I have my own ideas about things."

"What things?" he asked curiously.

"The way you should behave, and the way your dad should get on with his life and quit living in the past." She paused, wondering if her words were too harsh. "Look, Brad, maybe I'm just not the right woman for your father. I'm sorry," she sobbed, replacing the receiver, then making a dash to the ladies' room to dab at her watery eyes.

Returning, she paused beside Mona's desk, her chin thrust forward determinedly. "Please screen all my calls for the rest of the day."

"In other words, you don't want to talk to Brad Simpson," Mona replied nonchalantly.

"That's right." Casey picked at the lint on her dark dress. "Or his father. I can talk to them after working hours," she added briskly, then turned on her spiked heel and fled back to her desk. No doubt Mona thought she was behaving rather strangely, but she couldn't force herself to explain that those phone calls would only reduce her to tears.

Her request proved unnecessary. Brad did not telephone her again. Nor did his father. As her working days dragged by uneventfully, Casey felt a heavy weight around her heart, pulling her into a depression she couldn't shake.

Was Steve going to let it end like this? Was she?

She tossed and turned through sleepless nights, staggering into the kitchen in the mornings to pour coffee into her lethargic system. More pounds fell away, and her new wardrobe began to hang unattractively.

As the Thanksgiving holidays approached, Casey could scarcely force herself through her daily routine. Steve had just won a controversial case, which had earned headlines in the papers and been a topic of the evening news. As she sat before the warm lights flooding the news desk, reading from the Teleprompter, she stumbled over his name in reporting the trial. Afterwards, she made a dash back to her office, staring glumly at her desk.

Steve's face swam through her memory, his rich voice whispering through her consciousness. When she had angrily voiced her opinion and stormed out of his house that freezing night, she'd had no idea the break-up would cause such pain. She had replayed that scene a hundred times in her mind, convinced that she should have held her temper. And yet, she *had* spoken the truth. Patience, she reminded herself. They had been discussing patience that night before the argument began. She thought she had acquired patience over the years, but she realized now she had a long way to go.

Her telephone rang and she leaned forward to answer it, her weariness evident in her edgy voice.

"Casey?" At the sound of his voice, she bolted upright, all weariness forgotten.

"Steve." She tried to sound casual, but it was impossible. "How are you?"

"Tired," he sighed. "And you?"

"Tired," she nodded, her blond hair falling over her face. "Congratulations on winning the trial."

He hesitated, choosing his words carefully. "It was a stiff challenge, but one that I needed. At least it's kept my mind occupied—most of the time," he added, his emphasis not lost on Casey.

She sat rigid, her hopes building. "I've missed you," she said softly.

"I've missed you, too," he admitted, hesitating. "I couldn't let Thanksgiving pass without wishing you a pleasant holiday." The warmth had escaped his voice, replaced now by a new reserve. "Jane committed us to spending Thanksgiving with her, so we're heading up tomorrow."

"How nice," she replied tightly, suddenly angry beyond reason. "Have a good time," she added, too cheerfully.

There was a temporary silence before he cleared his throat and asked again, "How have you been?"

"Just *fine*," she thrust her chin forward, her voice firm and convincing.

"Well, good-by," he said tentatively, as though waiting for some further remark.

"Good-by." She hung up, wondering what more he had been expecting.

An apology?

Tears blurred her vision as she sat glaring at the phone. She was not too proud to admit her mistakes, but obviously *he* was. Nothing had changed, she realized, her spirits plummeting to rock bottom.

She prayed for wisdom and strength, and if there was a lesson to be learned in this heartbreak, she prayed that He would reveal that as well.

"It can't be *that* bad," a familiar voice drifted through her consciousness.

She looked up through misty eyes, her gaze focusing on Coy. She blinked, slow to recognize the man who stood before her.

"How was your vacation? Hey, you've lost weight." Her eyes widened in approval as she scanned his pressed Levis, crisp white shirt, neatly-trimmed beard and clean, styled hair. "My goodness, have you been promoted from cameraman to chief executive?" she asked with mock seriousness.

"Actually, I'm trying to replace a certain little co-anchor! There's a rumor going around that you and Simpson may be about to tie the big knot."

The glow in her eyes dulled as his words penetrated, and she felt her sudden good mood dissipating.

"Hardly." She looked away. "We've broken up."

He stared at her, the hazel eyes, narrowing as he considered her words. "I warned you—"

"I still think he's a wonderful man, Coy," she added quickly. "It's just that I'm too stubborn and he's too proud!"

Coy shifted his weight, regarding her curiously. "Listen, Green, if you really love the guy—and I know you do—you'd better think twice. I figure you've got pretty good judgment, after all, and if you saw enough in the guy to fall in love with him, you shouldn't be so quick to walk away."

"If it's meant to work out, it will. How's your family?" she asked, desperate for a change of subject.

He leaned down, planting his big palms on her desk. "Sharon and I are back together, Casey. And I have you to thank for it."

She stared at him, wide-eyed. "Coy, that's wonderful. But *I* had nothing to do with it."

"The Bible," he said huskily. "I've been reading the New Testament you gave me, and I'm here to tell you, I've been turned around from the old beer-guzzling, woman-chasing Coy!"

"I'm so happy for you, Coy!" she smiled brightly, studying the big man, so obviously changed.

"I'll bring your Bible back in a few days," he straightened. "Sharon is reading it now."

"Coy," she reached forward, gripping his hand, "keep it as a wedding present to you both. You *will* remarry, won't you?"

He shook his head. "Right away." He glanced nervously toward the rear of the newsroom. "Rosenthall's hawk-eyeing me. I'd better scoot. Remember what I said." The hazel eyes deepened with concern before he turned and bounded off, leaving Casey to ponder the meaning of his words.

If God could change a rebellious, hard-headed man like Coy Wilkens, couldn't He touch Steve as well, erasing all of his doubts and fears so that he could trust someone completely?

Someone!

The idea penetrated her mind like a steel-tipped arrow. What if he turned to another woman—a woman who was willing to take him without reservation, without commitment? A woman who would do as he suggested and hope for the best.

"Snap out of it," Mona nudged her. "You'll soon be going on the air. Better get some make-up dabbed on those sad eyes."

Casey turned to meet her friend's understanding gaze. "Yeah," she nodded, "the show must go on. Right?"

Casey accepted Ben's invitation to join him and his family for Thanksgiving dinner. His four children had provided lively entertainment for her, and while his house reverberated with joyful noise, his wife Anna did not seem to mind. Studying Anna's sparkling eyes and laughing face, Casey found herself questioning her own goals, her dubious successes. For the hundredth time.

As the holidays dragged by, Casey lounged on her living room sofa, staring at the silent telephone. Her fingers had reached out twice, aching to dial Steve's number, only to be halted by her fierce determination.

Stop that, she told herself. She would accomplish nothing by talking to him now. When they were both willing to compromise, they could talk. So far, she had not changed her mind. She still loved Steve, but she could not go on with their relationship until he came to grips with himself.

She slumped on the pillow, the old ache filling her being, as she stared glumly at the phone. To her astonishment, it rang.

She leapt forward, then struggled for composure. When she finally answered, a lady introduced herself as the senior editor of a prominent religious publishing house.

"We have a copy of the magazine article you wrote," she informed Casey. "And we think this story could be expanded into a remarkable book. This Sandra Billings seems to be the type of person who could be a real inspiration to our readers. Would you consider writing a book about her life?"

Casey's mouth dropped open, her mind groping for a reply. "I'm not really a writer," she began feebly.

"I disagree! You've written an exceptional article, Miss Green. Not only do you have a way with words, but you've managed to focus on the positive side of the woman's handicap, giving a fresh approach to this type of story. I can't believe you're an inexperienced writer," the woman countered pleasantly.

"Well, actually my experience is in television interviews," Casey admitted. "I think everyone has a story, no matter how unimportant they may feel it is—" she broke off, suddenly embarrassed by her chatty manner with this stranger.

"You see?" the editor pointed out, laughing. "This comes across in your writing, and you *are* a good writer. Are you interested in my offer?"

"I'd have to give it some thought," Casey replied uncertainly.

As they continued talking, the woman explained their plan for publishing the book, naming an impressive advance and assuring Casey the number of books printed would be worth her effort in terms of royalties. Further, she assured her there was a demand for this type of story, and that perhaps Casey could do additional work for them.

"Yes," Casey finally agreed. "I think I would like to try it."

After she hung up, Casey sat recalling her interviews with Sandy. The young woman attended her church, and Casey had been fascinated by her success in view of her severe handicap. Casey had gone to visit with her, and the lengthy visit had evolved in a magazine article.

She leaned her head against the sofa, her eyes drifting thoughtfully toward the ceiling. She recalled how easily Sandy had opened up to her, and how the joy of writing Sandy's story had made the work her most rewarding challenge in months.

Creative writing courses in college had been a great help in learning how to express herself. Perhaps she could even take some advanced courses in night school—

The idea of writing a book based on Sandy's life made Casey's adrenalin flow, and she leapt up from the sofa, pacing nervously. When she had weighed all the alternatives to a career in television, she had naturally considered a vocation dealing with people, yet she had been at a loss to think of another job where she could have the contact with people that she enjoyed as a reporter.

If she could establish herself as a writer, this would be work she could do at home. And she could be there for Steve and Brad. . . . She shook her blond head, attempting to shut out those thoughts. Her job wasn't the only problem in their relationship; therefore, she *must* make her decision independently of Steve.

Still, as Casey considered the idea of writing about people whose lives could be a source of encouragement to others, a smile formed on her lips. This could be the answer to her prayer!

When Casey received the contract for her book, she felt a sense of peace and relief. The publishing house had given her a flexible deadline and Sandra's enthusiasm about the project was infectious.

Casey lingered after church on Sunday for an appointment with her minister. In the privacy of his study, she had unburdened her heart, candidly revealing her love for Steve, along with her frustrations with her job, and her desire to write stories about people who could be a source of inspiration to others.

"Casey, I think God is already working this out for you." The understanding minister had looked at her, his gray eyes gentle and caring. "You've told me what you want to do. I just wonder if you've *heard yourself*."

"What do you mean?" she had asked, her dark eyes confused.

"You want to write inspiring stories and you want to marry Steve. You want to be a loving wife to him and a mother to Brad. Don't you realize that God is working in your life, as I'm sure he must be working in Steve's, as well?"

After a short prayer she had left the church, filled with assurance that God could change *her*, as well as Steve, shaping them into lifetime companions if they were willing to compromise.

On Monday morning she marched into Mr. Rosenthall's office and resigned, giving two weeks' notice. On Tuesday, she bought a new tape recorder and an electric typewriter. By Wednesday, the news had leaked out about her resignation and she spent the day attempting to answer questions while stubbornly clinging to her conviction that she had made the right decision.

Casey had been busy preparing for her new life—calculating how much she could live on and knowing she would have to live more frugally, yet still maintaining an aura of optimism and enthusiasm as anchor until she was replaced.

In all the excitement she had not failed to stop and stare longingly at the Christmas decorations going up across the city, her heart sending out a lonely cry when she thought of Brad and Steve, wondering how they would be spending Christmas.

On Saturday morning, as she was rummaging through her closet, selecting clothes to take with her to Texas for the brief holiday she planned to share with her parents, the doorbell rang. Struggling up from her position on the closet floor where she sat examining a pair of worn leather boots, she tossed a cursory glance down her jeans and sweatshirt, then lifted a hand to rake through her tousled hair.

She opened the door, expecting to find the postman with another package for which she must sign. Instead, she was looking up into the vivid blue eyes that could, in one split second, turn her world upside down.

CHAPTER 11

"HELLO, CASEY." He stood with his hands thrust deep into his overcoat pockets, his cheeks ruddy from the cold.

"Hello, Steve." Her voice was scarcely audible as her hungry eyes drank in every contour of his lean face, lingering on the tense jaw and jutting chin. He seemed to have lapsed back into the old seriousness, judging from the dark slash of brows, the set mouth, and finally the pained blue gaze. "Come in." She stepped back, opening the door wider.

"Were you busy?" he asked, hesitating.

"I was just trying to talk myself into cleaning some boots," she replied, giving a faint laugh.

He sauntered in, his gaze raking the apartment. When his eyes lingered on the kitchen, she knew he was remembering the meal he had prepared for her. She, too, was remembering and for a moment she was unable to think, to move, as she stood clutching the door facing, her eyes pinned to his back.

"You look cold," she said, closing the door before turning to face him. "How about some coffee?"

The deep blue eyes quietly searched her face before he answered. "Yes, thank you."

"May I take your coat?" She waited as he fumbled with the buttons. When she reached for it, their hands brushed, further unsettling her nerves. She felt him measuring her reaction, but she refused to lift her eyes to his, moving to hang the coat in the closet.

"Have a seat," she invited, disturbed by the polite, almost formal manner they were using.

She hurried into the kitchen, wondering why he had come. Her fingers fumbled with the spoon, then the canned coffee, her nervousness making her movements awkward as she struggled to count out the right number of spoonfuls. Plugging the cord into the outlet, she joined Steve in the living room.

Casey ran fingers through her hair, then made a futile effort to smooth her rumpled sweatshirt. Why had she given in to such sloppiness on her day off? she wondered angrily. Her appearance today was a complete departure from her usual impeccable neatness.

"I'm afraid I'm a mess," she forced a brittle laugh as she entered the living room. "I've been doing some cleaning." She swept a hand toward the living room. Well, at least her apartment was clean and in order for the first time ever. Had he noticed?

"Why did you quit, Casey?" he asked, the blue gaze directed at her face. "I just read about it in the morning paper." Steve had scooted to the edge of the sofa, his hands gripped tightly, as he waited for her answer.

She took a deep breath, crossing her arms and planting her feet firmly in the center of her worn carpet. She braced her knees, hoping to still their trembling.

"Steve, I told you, I wasn't happy with the job. What I liked best about reporting was my on-the-street interviews. I loved talking with everyday people, finding something inspiring about their lives. When I quit reporting and began sitting behind a desk, with hot bright lights in my face and a canned script in my hand, my work lost its appeal."

The pained expression on her face softened as a new glow filled her brown eyes, the gold flecks sparkling. "Now I've found a way to do enjoyable, rewarding work and still be a homebody—if I want to be," she added softly, letting the meaningful words drift between them.

His piercing blue gaze dropped to his clenched hands, as he became suddenly conscious of them, and he busied himself with dusting the leg of his business suit. "I see," he replied, in a tone that indicated he didn't understand at all. "What are you going to do now?" he asked, a worried frown knitting the dark brows together. "Will you be leaving Colorado Springs?"

"No," she shook her head. "I love it here, and I have no plans to leave."

"*Thank God!*" He released a heavy sigh, leaning back against the sofa. He looked across at her, the hard jaw slowly relaxing as she smiled in response.

"A religious publishing firm wants me to write a book on Sandy," she explained. "You remember—the handicapped artist I wrote about in the magazine article?"

At his affirmative nod, she continued, her voice ringing with enthusiasm. "I've signed a contract and, with the generous advance, I'll be able to manage nicely until the royalties come in. I'll begin working with Sandy after the holidays."

He stared at her in silence, obviously unconvinced that she was doing the right thing.

"Don't you see, Steve? I can write books about people whose lives are inspiring to others. It's worthwhile work—something I'll be proud to do—without sacrificing a home life." She leaned forward, intent on making him understand. "Believe me, I'm *certain* I've made the right decision."

He sat contemplating her words before nodding slowly. "You seem to be very confident. And I keep forgetting," he dragged his eyes away from her, concentrating on some distant object, "you aren't as materialistic as I've always been. In fact, I'm just realizing that the satisfaction you derive from your work is more important to you than the money *or* the recognition."

"That's right," she nodded, her eyes bright.

He swore under his breath, raking a nervous hand through his dark wavy hair.

"What's wrong?" she gasped. "You seem almost *angry* about my decision."

" Everything is so simple for you!" he turned back, the blue eyes stormy. "You say and do things with some kind of child-like—" he stumbled for a word.

"Faith," she inserted.

"Faith," he nodded, "that everything is going to work out just perfectly. It's as though you were completely ignoring the cold, hard facts of life."

She shook her head, confused. "But how does my faith in myself, in other people, *in God*, dispute the cold, hard facts? I think, Steve, you're *too* regimented. You see, I believe that when you live by faith, believing God's Word and accepting His promises, you can have what you seek—because what you seek will be a part of God's will for you. That's my philosophy. It's the way I've always lived." Her voice rose in conviction, her steady gaze confirming her words.

They stared at each other in silence, each trying to comprehend the other's viewpoint.

"The coffee—" she remembered suddenly, grateful for the distraction.

He followed her to the snack bar and sank down, propping his elbows on the counter as he watched her pull down mugs from the cabinet and pour the freshly brewed coffee.

"Why am I challenging that?" he asked finally, his voice softening in resignation. "Your philosophy works for you far better than mine has worked for me."

Her glance darted across to him, then back to the dark liquid filling the mugs.

"Do you really think my choices have been that uncomplicated, Steve?" she asked, taking the mugs across to the bar. She placed the steaming mug before him, facing him opposite the narrow ledge, her brown eyes meeting his.

He sipped his coffee thoughtfully. "No, I guess not."

"How's Brad?" she asked, a slight catch in her voice. "I've missed him."

He toyed with the handle of the mug as he sat staring into his coffee. "He misses you, *too*." The blue gaze slid back to her, the eyes deeply troubled, but he said nothing more.

She waited, every nerve in her body tensed for words that never came, until finally she could no longer bear the lengthy silence and grabbed at the first subject that popped into her head.

"Well, I'm finally going to visit my parents. For Christmas," she added, her throat aching. "I think they had just about decided their baby was never coming back, so I'll fly down Friday evening after my newscast. My last one," she added with a note of nostalgia.

"How long will you be staying?" he asked tightly.

She shrugged. "Since I'm self-employed now, I'm working my own hours. Hope that doesn't get to be a problem," she laughed nervously.

What am I babbling about? she wondered, feeling the old hurt creep in again. Neither of them cared about her new working schedule. All the things that mattered most were being left unsaid.

Steve glanced at his watch. "I'm due at the office in five minutes," he sighed. "Another challenge." He looked at her, the eyes bleak and dull.

She moistened her lips, her eyes clinging stubbornly to his face, refusing to let go.

"I'll have a gift for Brad. I haven't bought it yet, because there hasn't been time for Christmas shopping. But I'm going this evening. Tell me something he'd like." She swallowed, the memory of his appealing voice, his wide inquisitive eyes, his dark unruly hair forming an image in her mind that brought quick tears. She bit her lip, blinking, refusing to break down as Steve sat coolly watching her.

"He'd like to have you as a friend again," he said quietly.

"Again? I'll *always* be Brad's friend." She looked at Steve, startled.

He shrugged, standing to go. "He said when he called, you were very abrupt with him. He thinks you don't care about him anymore."

"That's not true," she gasped. "How could he possibly think that? And how could you?"

Casey came around the end of the bar, dazed, moving toward the closet to get his coat as her mind digested his hurtful words. As she pulled the heavy coat from the hanger, she clasped it tightly against her, as though by this act she could hold him longer.

She faced him, her wounded gaze seeking refuge in the blue eyes. He, too, was hesitating.

152

"All right, Steve, you win," she said, her voice trembling. "I'm not too proud to say it. I love you. I've never for one second stopped loving you. And I love Brad."

The sharp intake of his breath matched the sudden pain that filled his eyes as he clenched his jaw, refusing to answer.

"And I'm learning patience," she continued bravely. "I've done what I felt was necessary to mold my life to yours. I'm willing to wait until you can do the same for me."

In the next second he had closed the gap between them, wrapping her against him so tightly she could scarcely breathe, his warm mouth devouring her lips, leaving no doubt as to the raging hunger within.

"Oh, Casey," he moaned, pressing his hard jaw against her golden head. "I don't deserve you. God knows I don't. But I'm miserable without you!"

"Steve," she leaned her face against his chest, "don't ever say you don't deserve me. I'm not some goody-goody who has no conception of pain and heartache and disappointment." She swallowed, unable to stop the tears spilling down her cheeks. "I'm stubborn, I'm high-tempered, I'm impatient—maybe *I* don't deserve *you*!"

Gentle hands cupped her face, tilting her head back so that he could stare down into her wet face.

"You're all I could ever want in a woman. But don't you see?" The blue eyes were filled with an agony that stopped Casey's breath. "We *are* basically different," he said. "We *do* have different goals. I could never make a business decision based on some kind of faith."

"Steve, I'm not trying to change you," she sobbed. "Right now, I'm working on changing *me*. If we want to work out our problems, I know we can. But we both have to be willing to compromise."

153

The hands slid away from her face as he quietly reached for his coat, pulling it free of her grasp.

"Don't you think it would be easy for me to lie to you, to pretend belief in your God just to win you back?" He pulled on his overcoat, his mouth twisted in a grim line. "I've had enough guilt. I can't handle more."

"Because you feel your marriage was a failure?" she asked softly.

"That's one thing," he nodded. "I see so many things I should have done differently. After Scarlett became ill, I should have taken a leave of absence to be with her." He shook his head, remembering. "When she gave up her work, it was as though something inside her had already died."

His eyes were deeply haunted with a pain that was almost tangible as he continued, his voice strained.

"When I fell in love with you, I was too blind to see that I have to deal with things in my past before I could have a happy marriage. You were wise to point that out to me. At first, I didn't want to admit it. but since we've been apart I've had time to think everything out more logically. You were *right*," he stared down at her, the lean face drawn, "there are too many problems."

"Steve, I'm still willing to try," she swallowed, sensing she had begun to fight a losing battle. "I'll do my best to make it work."

He pressed her head to his chest, silencing her. "You don't understand. I admit that I wanted to marry you quickly before I had too much time to think. If you were lying beside me every night, I knew I could silence the nagging voices that keep reminding me: Scarlett is dead and I'm alive."

"Steve, you're wallowing in guilt." She pressed her hands against his coat, pushing back from him to look up into his tormented face. "*Why?*You're a good

154

father, even if you are a busy one. And despite what you're saying, I know you were a good husband, too. You're gentle, kind, understanding. Maybe you're a stickler for facts and logic in the courtroom, but you're different in matters of the heart. You said so yourself, remember?" she reminded him, hoping to lighten his dark mood.

He nodded, avoiding her pleading gaze. "I don't want to hurt anyone—"

"Steve, we all make mistakes," she reached for his hand, pressing it warmly between hers. "Scarlett would want you to be happy now. She would want Brad to have a mother, and I know she wouldn't expect you to waste the rest of your life grieving over her. It doesn't make sense!"

Gently he pulled his hands free, silently turning for the door. Casey stared after him, her heart breaking. How could she reach him? Even now, loving him as she did, she would rather see him happy with someone else than going through life all alone.

He paused at the door, his hand on the knob, his back stiffening.

"She was sick for a long time," his voice was low, muffled. "But she didn't die a natural death."

He opened the door slowly, never turning around.

"She committed suicide. I could have stopped her. I didn't."

The door clicked softly and he was gone.

CHAPTER 12

THE ROOM SWAYED as Casey gripped the back of the sofa, her face white, her eyes glassy with shock.

She stood staring at the closed door, mentally repeating the words Steve had spoken.

"Oh, dear God," she wailed, stumbling blindly around the sofa to sink into the cushioned softness before her knees buckled. She tried to think, to pray. But she was too numb.

Unable to react beyond a response to the hurt welling within her, she burst into sobs, her body heaving. Tears poured down her face, her neck, dampening her sweatshirt as she gave over to the terrible ache that filled up within her, begging for release.

When she thought back to that period of agony later, she had no idea how long she had sat crying. She only knew that it had taken a very long time to rid herself of the pain and frustration that had overwhelmed her. Then she had curled up in a ball on the sofa and dropped into a deep exhausted sleep.

She came awake slowly, her tangled lashes still matted from her tears. Just before she returned to full wakefulness, there was a dark cloud overhanging her memory. Remembering was painful and she fought it until her eyes fluttered open. Then Steve's haunting words rocked her in undulating waves of panic.

No, it couldn't be true! Steve would not have stood by and knowingly allowed his wife to commit suicide. He would never do that; so why did he lie to her?

She sat up, pressing her fingers to the throbbing ache in her temples. She blinked into the semi-darkness of the living room, determined to sort through the disturbing facts.

She had believed him earlier, and the pain of his words had produced hysteria. Now she leaned back against the sofa, trying to think rationally. She knew Steve too well to believe that he would do as he had said.

And yet—

The explanation made sense when she recalled Steve's attempts to bury himself in his work in order to escape . . . guilt? This guilt had even separated him from Brad, driving a wedge between them, one that Brad had failed to understand. Most of all, it explained his guilt in loving her.

No, she shook her head, dazed; it couldn't be true!

Ben had said Scarlett suffered from a rare disease. Casey remembered scraps of office gossip when she had come to work at the station, that the lovely model had endured great pain in the last stages of her illness. She frowned, trying to recall more. There were no other arguments to offset Steve's statement.

So, *how* had Scarlett died?

Casey pulled herself up from the sofa, stumbling into the bathroom to wash her face. Splashing cold water onto her swollen lids, she dried her face with a soft terry towel, her mind wrestling with a solution.

157

Somewhere between the bathroom and her bedroom, she knew what she must do. Remembering Steve was at the office, she sat down on the bed and reached for the telephone, dialing his home.

"Martha, I need to talk to you privately," she said shakily, as soon as the woman answered.

"Casey? Is that you?" Martha asked worriedly. "Oh, heavens yes, we do need to talk! Mr. Simpson and Brad are in a terrible state since—" she broke off, clearing her throat. "Brad is spending the afternoon with a friend, and Mr. Simpson is working late again. Could you come now?"

"Yes," Casey nodded quickly. "I'll be right over."

As Martha opened the door, Casey thought the older woman looked as distressed as she had the first afternoon Casey had come to visit—the day Brad had run away from home.

"Come in, dear." The housekeeper's soft tone brought a sigh of relief to Casey who had begun to suspect that, for some obscure reason, Martha had never accepted her, might still be blaming her for everything.

"I've made some coffee," Martha said, a warmth in her hazel eyes that had not been there before.

Passing the hall mirror, Casey was shocked at the sight of her own red eyes and pale face, despite her neatly brushed hair and change of clothes.

There was no point in trying to conceal her pain, Casey decided, following Martha to the kitchen. There had been too much waiting already, too many days of hiding grief and frustration. She thrust her chin forward, determined to seek the answers for which she had come.

Sitting down at the kitchen table, Casey tried to forget her last evening with Steve in this room. The memory of his strong arms about her, the glow of love in his eyes brought a stab of fear to her chest. What if he *had* allowed Scarlett to take her life, even encouraged it? some demon taunted. Casey blinked, forcing herself to seek the truth, whatever the cost.

"How have you been, Martha?" she asked, seeking to fill the silent void with idle conversation.

"Oh, I'm fine, I guess." Martha brought the coffee cups to the table and sat down opposite her. "But Mr. Simpson and Brad have been miserable. Casey, what on earth happened between you two?"

Casey stared down at the steam curling up from the hot coffee. "Martha, Steve and I broke up because he couldn't pull himself out of the past. To build a new life will take courage and faith—faith in himself, faith in our love, and—and faith in God."

She raised her pained eyes to meet the older woman's sympathetic gaze. "I love Steve and Brad very much," she swallowed, "but Steve has to solve some problems for himself before we could ever be happy together."

Martha nodded. "I know what you mean. There have been days when he has sat in the study all day long, just staring into space. I don't know why he took her death so hard," she sighed, "and please don't misunderstand what I'm saying. Naturally a man should grieve but," Martha shook her gray head, "to be perfectly honest, Casey, Scarlett was a very self-centered, vain woman."

Casey frowned, absorbing those words.

"If her hair didn't look just right, or if she couldn't buy the latest fashions, or if she and Mr. Simpson couldn't go to some big party, she pouted for days. She *was* a beautiful woman," Martha conceded, "but she certainly didn't have her priorities in order. She was very upset when she got pregnant with Brad, and

159

after he was born, she worried more about getting her figure back than nursing him through his colic."

Martha paused, sipping her coffee. "I spent a lot more time with Brad than she did. And Mr. Simpson got up with him for his two o'clock feeding. I shouldn't be saying these things about her since she's gone," Martha apologized quickly, "but I don't think Mr. Simpson would have ever married her if he had taken time to think about it. It was one of those whirlwind courtships. Scarlett was the type of woman who always got what she wanted—one way or another."

"I see," Casey nodded thoughtfully, so many missing pieces falling into place. "It's hard to imagine a person not appreciating Steve and Brad."

"I think it was because of the way *she* was raised," Martha explained, referring to Scarlett. "Her parents died when she was small. She went to live with an aunt who didn't give a hoot about her, from what Scarlett said. Yet Scarlett seemed to pattern herself after the aunt, who was also a very selfish woman. Odd, isn't it? They had a love-hate relationship most of her growing-up years, and yet she became just like the woman!"

"Sometimes that's the way it happens," Casey said, staring down at her coffee. "Martha," she looked up again, her eyes questioning, "how did she die?"

Martha's gaze widened in surprise. "Why, she had a rare form of cancer, didn't you know? I've forgotten the medical term, but it was a slow type where the muscles disintegrate. So sad!"

Casey nodded, recognizing the disease as the subject of a recent short feature.

"Did she die here at home?" Casey asked, her voice a mere whisper. "Was it a painful death? Were Brad and Steve with her?"

Martha lifted a hand to her forehead, pressing her fingers against her temples as though a headache were beginning. "She died in her sleep, thank goodness. The doctor had been here that day to bring more medication. That afternoon he told Mr. and Mrs. Simpson that it was just a matter of days."

"He told Scarlett?" Casey asked, surprised.

"Oh, yes! He was always honest with her. She wouldn't have it any other way," Martha explained quickly. "After he left, I heard Mr. and Mrs. Simpson arguing upstairs. Then Scarlett became hysterical. She did that a lot in those last days," Martha sighed. "Mr. Simpson came downstairs with the most pathetic look on his face. He went into his study and didn't come out for the rest of the evening.

"I put Brad to bed and left. When I arrived the next morning, Mr. Simpson was on the phone talking to the doctor. The poor man had been up most of the night. He said he couldn't wake Scarlett. When the doctor came and examined her, he said she had died in her sleep."

Casey leaned back in her chair, unable to comment as she stared at Martha.

"Here, let me freshen your coffee. You've let it get cold." Martha jumped up.

Casey nodded blankly, trying to piece the story together in her mind.

"Was Steve . . . terribly upset?" She turned in her chair, her eyes following Martha across the kitchen.

"He was devastated," Martha said, returning with the coffee. "It was almost as if he blamed himself, but there was nothing he could have done. I did hear the doctor say she had taken too much of the medicine, judging from the amount missing from the bottle. But he said her pain was probably so great that she wasn't responsible."

Casey reached for her coffee, needing the caffeine

to jolt her stunned senses. She felt as though every bone in her body had melted while she sat motionless listening to Martha, her attention riveted on every word.

After awhile, she placed the coffee mug on the table and looked evenly at the plump housekeeper. "If Scarlett did take too much medicine, why should Steve blame himself?"

"Why, I can't imagine!" she exclaimed. "Mrs. Simpson *always* took a lot of medicine. I'm not one to say what a person should or shouldn't do, but if I had been in her place, I would have wanted to stay as coherent as possible. Her husband and son needed her, and knowing there wasn't much time. . . ."

Martha shook her head, studying her plump hands, folded before her on the table. "But no one argued with Scarlett in those last days. She did what she wanted to do and nobody could stop her. Finally Mr. Simpson just gave up. He told me once, 'Martha, don't force her to take food or do anything she doesn't want to.' He said the pain became worse when she got upset."

Casey sighed, weighing those words.

"I can assure you of one thing," Martha patted her hand. "Mr. Simpson has no reason to feel guilty now. No man could have been more patient or more understanding than he tried to be with her. And it wasn't easy, let me tell you."

Martha lapsed into a melancholy silence, sipping her coffee thoughtfully.

"Martha, you'll never know how much this little talk has helped." Casey smiled at her, the brown eyes warm with affection. "I believe Steve and I can work things out now. With God's help, we *will* work it out," she smiled, her voice ringing with conviction.

"Casey," Martha raised troubled eyes to her, "I owe you an apology." She paused, suddenly embar-

162

rassed. "I hate to admit this, but in the beginning, I didn't trust you. You were," she hesitated, weighing her words, "too pretty—too nice—too good. I suppose I've become hardened through the years. It was difficult for me to believe—well, that you were as sincere as you seemed." She studied Casey's worried face. "Then I got a little jealous," she grinned sheepishly, "seeing how Brad adored you. I'd never been able to win him over like that."

"Martha, Brad thinks of you as part of his family! I know he loves you, whether he shows it or not." Casey assured her.

Martha nodded, studying her coffee again. "Probably. But I'm ashamed now for acting so petty toward you. I realize that you're the very one to handle Brad—and Mr. Simpson, too, for that matter."

The front door slammed, startling them both.

Martha glanced nervously at the kitchen clock. "Mr. Simpson said he wouldn't be home until dinner time. And that's another thing," she frowned at Casey. "He's burying himself in his work again."

"I know," Casey sighed, saddened by the fact that work had seemingly become Steve's comforter, his escape, his release from pain.

Brad pushed through the kitchen door, his expression brightening at the sight of Casey.

"Well, hello, Brad!" Casey gave him her widest smile, her eager gaze running over his loose sweat-shirt, his faded Levis and scuffed-up tennis shoes.

"Casey!" He bounded into her arms, almost squeezing the breath from her body.

She gasped but hugged him back enthusiastically. "I came to tell you the good news." She lifted his chin to look into the blue eyes, tiny replicas of his father's.

"What good news?" he asked suspiciously.

163

"I'm quitting my job as anchor! Now I can take you to Sunday school again."

"*You can*?" His little face glowed with happiness. "And you're not mad at me—or at Dad?" he asked nervously.

"Honey, I was never mad at you. I'm very sorry if you ever thought I was. And I'm not mad at your father, either." She patted his dark head. "It's just that, well, I had to straighten some things out so we could spend more time together. I'm going to be working at home now, doing some writing. I'll still have a job, but not one that will keep me from doing things with you."

"Super!" he shouted. "Isn't that super, Martha?" he looked at her for approval.

"Yes, it is," Martha laughed, her hazel eyes glowing at the sight of his happy face.

"So are we going to Sunday school tomorrow?" he asked, fidgeting.

Casey sighed. "I had to swap mornings with my Sunday replacement so he could go to a special family reunion in Illinois. I'm working tonight and tomorrow. But after Friday, I won't be working at the station anymore."

"Can you stay and eat hamburgers?" Brad asked in a characteristic change of subject.

Casey glanced at the clock, aware that she would have to sprout wings and fly if she were to get back to her apartment and be dressed in time for her newscast.

"I can't. In fact, I'm already running late. But, Brad, you be a good boy this week. When I quit work, we'll do lots of things together."

"And I won't act up anymore just to get my way," he promised, throwing his arms around her waist.

The poignant words brought an ache to her throat as she hugged him. "I'm glad to hear you say that,

164

Brad. Sometimes pain and disappointment are necessary to teach us a lesson. Maybe we've all learned something."

"Everyone except Dad," he mumbled.

Casey nodded, sighing. "He'll learn in time, Brad. I just know it."

CHAPTER 13

"Well, I can see I have a real challenge cut out for me." A deep voice brought Casey upright.

She turned from her work-cluttered desk to the stranger standing beside her.

"You must be Walt Pennington," she extended her hand, smiling.

"Your replacement," he nodded, gripping her hand.

He was short, slightly built, with sandy blond hair, friendly green eyes and an extra-wide smile. There was a twinkle in the eyes that promised to steal a television audience as quickly as possible.

"Welcome to WJAK," Casey said, "you'll like it here." Her blond hair bounced with her affirmative nod.

"I'm sure I'll like *them*, but will they like *me*? Your faithful audience, I mean. You're leaving some pretty big shoes to fill, you know." His interested gaze ran the length of her tailored suit, returning to the silk blouse that brought out the gold flecks in her brown eyes.

She laughed softly. "I'm afraid the public is quite fickle, Walt. They'll miss me at first—maybe. But in a few days they'll have forgotten all about Casey Green."

"I doubt that." His brows arched in surprise. "You're much too pretty to forget."

She looked away, wishing he were not so determined to impress her. It really didn't matter what *she* thought of him, so why was he so eager to win her approval?

"How can I help?" Her tone was matter-of-fact.

"I understand Mr. Rosenthall has a rather unique little stunt planned for us. We're both to be interviewed on the final wrap-up of the news this evening."

"Oh, really?" Her eyes widened. "No one told me." She tried to hide her irritation.

"Well, they just told *me*. That's why I hustled on up to your office to get to know you first."

"I see." She looked at him thoughtfully.

While she appreciated Walt's friendliness, she was beginning to feel a little overpowered by his bold appraisal and his take-charge attitude. But, she reminded herself sharply, there were a few days remaining in her contract and she wanted to exit gracefully, helping Walt as much as possible, while being cooperative with the rest of the crew. She could afford to overlook the new man's aggressive manner, along with any of Mr. Rosenthall's little brainstorms.

The idea of being her own boss, working her own hours, doing her own thing brought a sigh of bliss to Casey's lips, and she lifted her brown eyes to Walt and actually smiled.

"Would you have time for a cup of coffee?" His gaze dropped to her desk, examining the sheaf of papers before her. "I'd like to go over some of the procedures with you if you can spare the time," he added lightly, assuming that she could.

"I'll take the time," she nodded agreeably, pushing her work aside.

She led the way through the busy newsroom, down the corridor to the coffee shop, conscious that Walt's eyes had never left her. She glanced up at him, realizing that he was only a few inches taller than she—five-eight, five-nine at the most. She had grown so accustomed to Steve, tall and broad-shouldered, that she found it a strange sensation to walk beside a shorter man.

"Where is your home?" she asked conversationally.

"Minneapolis—land of long cold winters."

"Welcome to more winter," she laughed, "only our snow is light and dry—quite different from yours."

"Yeah, the humidity is what kills you." He pushed the door open for her and they entered the small coffee shop.

As they seated themselves and ordered coffee, Casey tried to offer as many helpful suggestions as possible, pointing out the quirks in the news director's temperament, along with some tips for staying on the right side of certain cameramen.

"Well," Walt glanced at the slim gold watch on his wrist, "I can see this is going to be different from Minneapolis, but I think I'll like it."

"You will," she assured him. "So, let's get back upstairs and make our preparations for that interview. I need to be getting ready for the newscast, as well."

"Yes," he nodded, the green gaze sliding over her boldly. "You must knock 'em dead every evening."

"Not really." she replied stiffly. "Shall we go?"

"Stay tuned for the latest update on tomorrow's weather." Tim, Casey's co-anchor, looked into the camera as a lovely young woman popped up on the monitor, enticing the audience to try her favorite shampoo.

The cameramen wheeled their cameras toward the weather set, where the weatherman stood before his colorful map, adjusting his tie. Meanwhile Casey unhooked her microphone and hurried across to the interview set where Walt was chatting pleasantly with one of the cameramen, attempting to make himself at home.

"You know you're breaking our hearts, don't you?" The floor director came forward and placed a restraining hand on her arm. "How can you possibly leave us?"

"Oh, Tommy," she looked at him affectionately, "Walt will do a fine job. And just think, you won't have to suffer heart failure every time I stumble over a word!"

"Well," he grinned at her, "your good looks make up for that. Anyway, better hurry and get wired for the interview. Your replacement is chomping at the bits to get on camera," he whispered under his breath.

Casey rushed over to the sofa and took her seat, yanking at the hem of her skirt as the bright glare spotlighted them.

"Stand by. We'll be coming to you immediately after the commercial," a technician advised.

"Walt, want to give us a mike check?" a voice boomed beyond the glare of lights.

"Hello, everyone. I'm Walt Pennington." His resonant baritone filled the room.

"Terrific. Casey?"

"One, two, three . . . okay?" She squinted into the glare, something inside her refusing to take Walt's lead.

"Okay for both of you. Stand by—"

Clipping the microphone to the lapel of her suit, Casey leaned back on the sofa, glancing thoughtfully across at Walt, who was busily smoothing a tiny wrinkle from his immaculate dark business suit.

What Mr. Rosenthall wanted was an informal session with Casey introducing Walt as her replacement, and the two of them providing a down-home atmosphere to ease the transition before Walt's unfamiliar face appeared on the screen each evening.

"Ready on Camera One," a voice instructed, as Casey lifted a hand to smooth her blond hair, then turned to Walt, her mind quickly assimilating the facts about him.

As the red light above the camera flashed on, she looked directly into its magnetic eye and said cheerfully, "Good evening, folks. Tonight we're departing from our regular schedule. We at Channel Six would like to introduce you to the newest member of our team, Walt Pennington."

She turned to him as the camera zeroed in on them, capturing Walt's brilliant smile and practiced blue twinkle.

"Walt comes to us from Minneapolis and will be my replacement."

As they progressed with the segment, Walt took over easily, relating interesting bits of information about himself. Then, as planned in the closing seconds, Casey turned back to the camera, a sad smile on her pretty face. "I've loved every minute of being a part of the news team, and I hope you'll give Walt the love and encouragement you've always given me—"

To Casey's horror, her voice broke and a quick-thinking technician panned the camera back to a surprised Walt, who demonstrated the spontaneous recovery that had earned him the job.

"And, Casey, we'll all miss you," Walt gave the

170

camera his widest smile. "This is Walt Pennington, Channel 6 News. . . ."

Casey was at a loss for words, momentarily overcome with nostalgia, as she recalled the many friends here who had been kind to her. While she had no regrets about her decision, she realized that she should have been prepared for her sentimental nature to prevail in the end.

She was suddenly surrounded by co-workers, wishing her well and shoving handkerchiefs at her. Her wet eyes widened as Mr. Rosenthall loomed out of the crowd, assisting her from the sofa.

"There, there," he patted her shoulder. "We're planning a special good-by celebration for you at the end of the week, but for tonight, I've reserved a table for you and Walt at Howard's. Go on over there and have a nice dinner, compliments of WJAK."

"Oh, I—I don't think," she stammered, only to have her weak protest waved aside.

"Thank you, Mr. Rosenthall." Walt lunged forward, gripping the older man's hand. "I accept for both of us. That's very kind of you. And no arguments from you, Miss Green," Walt threatened, grinning. "We shouldn't take Mr. Rosenthall's good intentions lightly," he whispered, his hand on her elbow, as he steered her around the cable cord toward the back exit.

"This really isn't necessary." She wiped her eyes with a borrowed handkerchief as they made their way back to the newsroom.

"Of course it is," Walt argued. "You've earned yourself a fine meal at Howard's. We're crazy not to take advantage of Mr. Rosenthall's generosity."

"Oh, all right," she sighed, too drained for further objections.

As they left the building, Casey found herself unable to resist Walt's comforting arm around her shoulder. Still, she found herself wishing the man beside her were Steve, not some stranger from Minneapolis!

"Yes, my lady, we'll have a meal fit for a king—and queen," he teased.

Casey lifted her blurred eyes to the darkened parking lot, squinting toward the rows of parked cars. She almost didn't see him, yet a movement at the periphery of her vision alerted her to a familiar figure. She inclined her head to the left, and her gaze locked with a pair of shocked blue eyes.

"Steve!" she called to him, just before he turned to go. "Steve, wait!"

"Who?" Walt whirled, curious.

"Steve," she repeated, her heels clicking across the parking lot as she hurried to his parked car. He stood by his open door, preparing to leave.

"Hello," she said breathlessly as she reached him, her head tilted to look up into his dark face, his lean jaw jutting ominously.

"Hello," he replied, after he had looked long and deep into Casey's face. "I just stopped by on my way home, but I see you're busy." His gaze shifted to a spot above her head, probing Walt's face.

"Oh, Steve," Casey motioned a puzzled Walt closer, "this is my replacement, Walt Pennington. Walt, Steve Simpson."

"Nice to meet you," Walt stepped forward, extending his hand.

Steve shook hands abruptly, the dark brows lowered.

"Er, Steve," Walt accurately perceived the situation and offered a perfunctory invitation, "we were just going to dinner at Howard's. Won't you join us?"

Walt's attempt at friendliness failed to placate a sullen Steve, whose dark face became an angry mask.

"I have to get home. I just stopped by to thank you

172

for coming to see Brad." He looked at Casey, his gaze narrowing before he slid under the wheel of his car.

Casey took a step forward, her hands clenched at her sides. She wanted to throw herself into his arms, or, at the very least, lift a hand to soothe the troubled frown from his forehead.

"How did your case turn out?" she asked, suddenly remembering.

"I lost," he said, slamming the door, cranking the engine, then speeding out of the parking lot.

Walt whistled softly. "Now there's a jealous man if ever I saw one! Sorry if I caused problems. I didn't know. . . ."

She shook her head, shivering into her coat, as her brown eyes followed the big car out of sight. "I really don't think he wanted company, anyway."

Feeling utterly miserable, she turned back to Walt.

"I'm sorry, Walt, but I just don't feel like partying."

"You two are in love, aren't you?"

"Yes, but we certainly seem to be having our share of problems," she sighed. "Thanks for understanding, Walt. I think I'll go on home now." She felt as though a terrible weight had settled over her and it required great effort to drag herself across the parking lot.

"I'll walk with you," Walt offered, trailing after her. "Sure you don't want me to help you forget him?"

"I appreciate the offer," she forced a smile. "But I do love him, and I have faith that everything will work out for us—eventually," she added softly. "Good night."

The remainder of her week raced by, the winding-up of last-minute details crowding Steve from Casey's mind until she crawled into bed each night, aching with exhaustion. Then she would think of him, memories tearing her apart.

Father, she prayed, *please give me patience and understanding. And please touch Steve's heart. Let him accept Your forgiveness and Your love. In Jesus' name.*

Filled with a sense of peace, Casey closed her eyes, knowing that the God who was big enough to create the universe could create a new heart in the man she loved.

CHAPTER 14

CASEY TRUDGED OUT of the department store into the crowd of shoppers, her arms filled with gaily wrapped packages, her eyes staring unseeing at colorful shop windows.

She had labored long and hard over her Christmas list, finally deciding on the appropriate gifts for her family in Texas. Now, after hours of wandering through stores, she had completed her shopping.

Christmas carols rang out from the record shop she passed as she plodded along, her feet aching in the leather boots, her body shivering in her camelhair coat.

A cold wind had whipped down from the north during the afternoon, bringing the promise of snow. But for now the streets were merely rain-slickened, with the lowering temperature slowly icing car windows and pavements.

She paused at the street corner, waiting for the traffic light to change. A couple jostled carelessly against her, their lively voices attracting her curious gaze.

The girl's russet head was nestled against a sturdy shoulder; the man's arm around her protectively, as if to hold the chill wind at bay.

"You don't really want to be Christmas shopping with me," she teased.

"Hey, I wouldn't be anywhere else," he argued, leaning down to kiss her red mouth.

Casey looked away, embarrassed to be witnessing their intimacy.

"Christmas is a time of love, remember?" His voice was amplified by the crisp night air. "And when a guy loves someone, he wants to be with her."

Those words produced a pain in Casey's heart that was almost physical. Tears sprang to her eyes. Naturally, people in love wanted to be together at Christmas—shopping for presents, planning festivities, dreaming dreams. *And when a guy loves someone, he wants to be with her.* The words drummed through her tormented mind like a death march, louder and louder, until she had a strong compulsion to drop her packages and cover her ears, shutting out the sound of happy voices and Christmas bells and lilting carols.

The traffic light changed and she was only vaguely conscious of the milling crowd. Quickening her steps, she merged with the throng of shoppers crossing to the next block.

Maybe Steve doesn't really love you, after all! a mocking voice taunted. But she had tried so hard to win his love, to prove to him that she would be a good wife. Still, he had not responded. He had even failed to return her phone call today.

Recalling his angry face in the parking lot a few nights ago, Casey had finally swallowed her pride and called his office. Since she had made plane reserva-

176

tions for a Sunday afternoon flight to Texas, she wanted to see him once more before she left town. When the secretary informed her that Steve was out of the office but would be returning soon, she left her name and number. A couple of hours later she called again. The secretary explained that Steve and his son had just left for his condominium in Vail . . . and yes, she *had* given him the message.

Angered, Casey had pulled on her boots and coat, hoping that Christmas shopping would ease her troubled mind. But it had only made her more keenly aware of Steve's absence.

Maybe it really is over, she thought, pain searing her heart. *Maybe I'm just too stubborn to admit it*!

Oblivious to those who bumped against her, oblivious now to the Christmas music and softly ringing bells, she moved aimlessly, lost in a private world of agony.

She turned up the narrow side street leading to the parking lot, her mind numb, her hopes dying when she counted the days and nights she had not heard from Steve. *God, I don't know what else to do*, Casey cried from the depths of her heart.

Icy rain began to pelt down, yet Casey's feet dragged, her body refusing to hurry through the night, as the rain mingled with the tears dripping down her cold cheeks.

Glancing absently right and left, noting the scant flow of traffic, Casey decided to jaywalk after the last car passed. The rain was coming down harder now, and her thoughts were centered on getting to the parking lot before she got soaking wet.

She stepped off the curb, indifferent to the flash of car lights turning down the block, as one of the bulging sacks loosened in her arms. She paused to get a tighter grip. Then, aware of the approaching car, she quickened her pace, finally breaking into a run.

Halfway across the street, the heel of her right boot caught on some small object, throwing her off balance. Her body lunged backward, then forward, as she struggled to regain her footing without dropping her packages. The soles of her boots were too slick to give her the grip she needed, and she plunged headlong into the mud, her packages flying out of her arms.

A scream ripped from her throat as she lay helplessly watching the scene unfold before her, everything moving in a kind of lurid slow motion. The car swerved sideways . . . tires screeched . . . the pungent smell of burning rubber filled her nostrils . . . the sweep of headlights silhouetted her body . . . and, finally, the sickening impact of the fender against her side, as she involuntarily curled into a ball, her arms flung over her head.

Then darkness obliterated all reality, bringing a blessed cessation of the searing pain.

"Casey . . ."

A voice whispered in her ear, a gentle familiar voice that beckoned her from the eerie darkness enveloping her.

She tried to move, but her body failed to respond. She tried to open her eyelids, but the effort was useless. She struggled to speak, yet she could not force a single word past the thickness of her tongue.

"Casey . . ."

The voice floated through her darkness again, a soft pleading tone that tugged at her subconscious. The voice was one to which she had long responded, a voice that had spoken love and guidance through many years.

"Mom . . ."

The word finally penetrated the cotton in her mouth, fighting its way over her leaden tongue.

"Oh, baby! We've been so worried!"

Worried! Why was her mother worried?

She drifted back into the soft darkness that kept claiming her, the image of a young girl dancing through her mind—a girl surrounded by dolls and tea-sets, soothed by her mother's soft voice.

Then suddenly her big brother, Bobby, was there, yanking at her pigtails, teasing her until her mother's voice intervened, her tone mildly reproving.

Casey floated along on the dark sea of nothingness until another girl sprang to her subconscious, an older girl who wore braces and worried about dates for church picnics and school functions.

"No one ever asks me out," the girl complained, staring dismally into her mirror. The glass reflected the image of a thin little body, ugly braces, and an unruly ponytail.

There was that comforting voice again, warm and reassuring: "Someday there will be a wonderful man who will love and accept you for the beautiful person you are."

A tiny frown rumpled Casey's forehead, the words inducing a strange ache in her heart, an ache born out of some deep hurt that pulled her further into the darkness.

"Casey . . ."

The voice in her ear now was somehow connected with the pain, and she shuddered involuntarily. She felt the pain now, within and without, as she tried in vain to move against something light and crisp on her skin.

Slowly her eyelids fluttered open. She was enveloped in a world of white. White bed, white ceiling, white walls.

179

The pressure on her wrist increased. A hand gripped hers.

When she tried to turn her head, a blinding spasm seared a path behind her eyes, and she moaned softly.

"Easy, honey."

Her mother appeared in her line of vision, her small face lined with concern. Her short, gray-brown hair was brushed back in waves, and her brown eyes were moist as though she had been crying.

"Hello darling." She leaned down and kissed Casey's cheek.

"Mom, where am I?" she asked weakly.

"In the hospital, honey," her mother replied softly. "You were hit by a car. You have a slight concussion and some broken ribs, but you're going to be fine." The gentle voice trembled on those last words.

Casey blinked at the ceiling, her mind creeping back to the events of the rainy night. She remembered stepping down from the curb, hurrying across the street . . . then the fall . . . and the car! She bit her lips to stifle a scream as the scenario replayed itself in her mind.

"Just relax, Miss Green." A nurse appeared at her side, brown eyes scrutinizing her from beneath a crisp white cap. Her cool fingers encircled Casey's limp wrist as the nurse stared down at her watch, counting. When the vital signs were recorded, she held a straw to Casey's parched lips. "Slowly now. Just a sip at first."

Casey obeyed, relishing the cold water on her tongue while her eyes searched her sterile surroundings. A small narrow tube led from a needle in her arm to a jar suspended overhead.

"How long have I been here?" Casey asked after the water trickled down her throat.

"You were admitted last night." The nurse wound

a wide band around her arm, checking her blood pressure. "You're doing fine. Just keep still."

Casey nodded, then flinched at the pain.

The nurse retreated and her mother stood over her again.

"The man who hit you was one of your fans, Casey. He was completely broken up about the accident. He followed the ambulance to the hospital, then called the television station. When Ben Steele notified us, we took the first plane out." Her mother patted her arm, but Casey had the feeling that *she* was the one who needed consoling.

Casey blinked up at her, trying to make sense of everything.

"I . . . had planned to spend Christmas in Texas," Casey sighed. "I'm sorry."

"Don't apologize, honey! Your father and I are just so very grateful—" she choked, shutting off the words. "You had a close call, Casey. But the Lord was with you," Ruth Green smiled down at her daughter. "I have to leave now. In Intensive Care, visitors are allowed in for only a few minutes. Try to rest now." She patted her arm again.

"I will," Casey replied, closing her eyes. She was conscious of the dull throbbing in her head. She felt very tired and weak. But just before sinking into a deep sleep, she thought of Steve Simpson. A terrible sadness engulfed her, intensifying the pain in her head.

Sometime later Casey was aware of a numbness in her legs when she tried to move. Lifting her head to look down at her feet, the white world rolled and a wave of nausea swept her.

"Just lie still, Miss Green," a nurse admonished, "you mustn't move your head."

"My legs," Casey replied weakly. "I have no feeling in my legs!"

The woman's eyes darted down the still form. "Just try to rest," she said. "The doctor will talk to you in the morning."

Casey stared at the nurse, her mind struggling to comprehend. Was she deliberately being evasive?

"Is there something wrong with my legs?" Casey pressed. "I can't feel anything!"

"Miss Green, I really can't say," the nurse replied, her tone sympathetic, but carefully noncommittal. "Perhaps it's the medication."

Casey thought about that as the nurse disappeared from her line of vision. Although she knew she had sustained a brain concussion, her head didn't feel numb. Only her legs and feet. She tried to wiggle her toes, but she couldn't tell if anything moved.

A cold fear gripped her, a fear unlike anything she had ever known. *Was she paralyzed?*

"Time for your shot." The nurse was back with a hypodermic. Casey scarcely felt the sharp prick in her arm as her mind struggled with the awesome horror of paralysis.

She thought of Sandy, her handicapped friend who had spent her life in a wheelchair. She felt such empathy for Sandy now. For the first time in her life, she knew the desperation of complete helplessness. How, she wondered bleakly, had Sandy triumphed over her handicap with such warmth and cheerfulness?

The numbness in her legs was creeping through the rest of her body now. She closed her eyes, welcoming the blessed relief of the sedative.

Throughout the night, Casey slipped in and out of consciousness, awakened by the nurses' perfunctory checks. During those wakeful moments, she was aware of the lingering numbness in her lower body. Somewhere in the darkness of her mind, Steve hovered, his face appearing before her, then disappearing just as she reached out for him.

"Miss Green?"

Casey tried to swim up from the deep darkness that claimed her. She felt a strong hand on hers; firm fingers encircled her wrist.

She pushed against the weight of her eyelids until finally her eyes focused on the face of a strange man. A man with white hair and compassionate hazel eyes.

"Good morning, Miss Green. I'm Doctor Wallace. If you could wake up for a few minutes, I'd like to talk with you."

Casey tried to swallow but her mouth was too dry. A nurse appeared, inserting a straw between her lips. "Slowly now," the nurse smiled.

The cool water restored her momentarily, and forgetting her condition, she tried to sit up. Firm hands gripped her shoulders, easing her back onto the pillow.

"Just lie still." The doctor's tone was firm, yet his smile was gentle. "You're doing very well."

Casey tried to wiggle her toes. Nothing happened.

"Doctor, I have no feeling in my legs or feet," she said shakily.

"It's the medication," he replied confidently. "We've had to sedate you in order to keep your head still because of the concussion. I can assure you there is no damage to your spinal cord."

"But I thought—" she broke off uncertainly.

"And your thoughts made it worse," he nodded. "Don't worry, young lady. The feeling will return to your lower body sometime today. I'm cutting back on the medication. In fact, I'm even thinking of moving you out of Intensive Care into a private room. Would you like that?"

She stared at him, scarcely able to believe her ears.

"Yes. Thank you. I'd like that very much," she managed to reply.

Just as the doctor had predicted, the feeling returned to her legs later that day. Casey was so relieved that she wept with joy. Never would she forget the tormented night she had spent, fearing that she was paralyzed. Nor would she forget her feelings of empathy for Sandy, and for all handicapped people. She knew, now, that her story of Sandy's life would be stronger, better. For she had experienced for one horrifying night the emotions of a person handicapped for life.

She moved her head slowly, glancing appreciatively at her comfortable room filled with lovely bouquets of flowers. Her accident had made the six o'clock news the previous evening, and now devoted friends and fans had sent tangible evidence of their love and encouragement. She felt proud and, at the same time, humble. It touched her to know so many people were concerned for her.

But there had been no word from Steve and Brad.

She sighed, turning toward the window that looked out on Pikes Peak to the west. The snowstorm that had dumped three feet of snow on the city had stopped all traffic in the higher elevations. If Steve and Brad were still in Vail, they would be unable to return to Colorado Springs now that the roads were closed—even if they wanted to.

"Anyone home?" Ben Steele tapped on her door, then without waiting for a reply, pushed it open. "And just what are you doing here?" he asked with mock severity. "You see, you should never have left us. We took much better care of you."

Casey laughed softly. "Come in, Ben. How are you?"

"Obviously better than you!" He strode across the room, peering down at her through his horn-rimmed glasses.

"I'm going to be all right," she assured him. Then, abruptly, "Look at all the flowers my fans sent. Aren't they lovely?"

Ben turned, flicking a quick glance over the fragrant room.

"Which only proves my point," he replied.

"Your point?" she blinked.

"That you should come back to the station. Your fans miss you. We all miss you."

"I think you're the nicest man I know, Ben Steele! Thank you for saying that."

"You know I'm *never* nice," he protested, thrusting his hands into his overcoat pocket. "Actually, the phone calls are pouring in at WJAK. In addition to the fans' concern for your health, we're getting a rash of complaints for letting you get away in the first place! How about it, Casey? Would you consider coming back—with, uh, an increase in pay, of course."

Casey stared at her boss, wondering. *Would* she consider resuming her career now that Steve was out of her life?

"What about Walt Pennington?" she asked. Walt would not be one to relinquish his new position easily.

He snorted impatiently. "Doesn't have your appeal."

"Why not, Ben? He seems tough enough. Remember you always said I needed to be tougher—that I'd never make it in television if I took things too seriously."

"All right—all right." He threw up a hand to

185

silence her. "You know I never like to be reminded when I'm wrong—which doesn't happen often," he added, pausing to rake his hand through his thinning dark hair. "But you have a very special quality that draws people to you," he conceded. "Now this obvious concern for the man on the street wouldn't work for everyone, but—well—it works for you. I'm glad you didn't take my advice, kid!"

She smiled sadly, her gaze traveling over the flower-filled room.

"Think it over," he tapped her arm. "The job is still yours if you want it."

"I don't know, Ben. But I *will* think about it."

"Did your parents come up from Texas?" Ben asked.

"Yes, they did. I'm surprised you didn't trip over them in the hallway. They've haunted the hospital night and day. Now that Mom and Dad are convinced I'm going to survive, they're finally getting some rest."

"Well, take care, Casey. And promise me you'll think about my offer." Ben paused at the door.

"I'll think about it."

Hearing Ben's steps echoing down the corridor, she considered his words again. Without Steve and Brad, she felt a terrible void in her heart. She was going to do the book on Sandy, of that she was certain. Perhaps she could also consider going back to work. Maybe the flowers and messages from her fans were proof that she *was* bringing a fresh and needed approach to news coverage.

She turned on her side, gazing out at the snow-covered mountain range. Again she thought of Steve, recalling the day they had strolled through the streets of Vail, hand-in-hand, as thrilled over the falling snow as a couple of kids.

186

The words he had spoken that day drifted back through her mind, bringing an ache to her heart.

"Your faith is as strong as that mountain," he had said with a hint of grudging respect—and perhaps envy—in his voice.

But her faith was not that strong, she was forced to admit. What had happened to her stubborn determination to cling to God's promises? To accept His will for her life without question? In order to do that, she had to believe, even now, that all things would work for her good.

How could the accident possibly be for her good? How could knowing and loving Steve, then losing him, work for her good?

She sighed, drained of tears. She had been so certain that her faith could overcome the obstacles in their relationship. But she realized now that she had been pursuing her own selfish desires. Even her prayers had been directed toward changing *Steve,* toward leading him into *her* faith.

Swallowing against the ache in her throat, she gazed at towering Pikes Peak, longing to be as unswerving in her faith as this mountain that had survived the storms of many winters and emerged, lovelier than ever, with each new spring. The mountain did not resist the laws of nature. It simply endured.

A Christian needed that kind of acceptance of God's will to withstand troubled times. God had always done what was best for her. She knew that now. Why had she tried to make everything work the way *she* wanted it to? Perhaps her purpose in knowing Steve and Brad had already been fulfilled.

She closed her eyes, searching her soul for answers, but there were none. Finally, her pale lips parted and she whispered a soft prayer. "God, I accept Your will for my life. Whatever it is. And I thank you that You will do what is best, that I have that assurance. It makes no difference that I don't understand every-thing, or that I feel hurt—even a little angry—right now. I know that in time You will replace those emotions with the complete peace that only You can give."

Slowly, the softness of a snowy mountain evening settled over her room. Faraway lights twinkled along the skyline, bringing a glow of comfort to Casey as she drifted off to sleep—a peaceful, contented sleep.

When Casey looked into her hand mirror the next morning, she was appalled to discover the dark circles under her sunken eyes. She looked up at her mother, busily arranging Casey's cosmetics on the table nearby.

"Mom, the gown helped," Casey glanced down at the frilly blue nylon gown and robe, "but it's going to take a ton of make-up to brighten my face!"

"Nonsense," her mother smiled encouragingly. "You look lovely, dear. Besides, that special shade of blue makes your eyes sparkle. And your hair is much prettier since we brushed out all the tangles." Her mother glanced at the telephone by the bed. "This should lift your spirits—we're reconnecting the phone today. The doctor ordered it unplugged until you were up to taking calls. I think the nurses' station is being swamped with messages," she laughed. "Perhaps *they* suggested you have your own phone now."

Casey nodded, hoping the doctor would decide to take the IV out of her arm. She was so tired of being confined to the bed.

"Well," her mother glanced approvingly at the room, "now that I've tidied up, I'm going to meet your father for lunch. He's been prowling around the newsstands downstairs, exhausting their supply of city papers."

Casey glanced toward the window. Bright sunshine greeted her, and while the Peak was still covered with snow, the temperature appeared to be climbing back up to normal.

"Is it cold outside?" she asked her mother.

"Not too cold. The streets are cleared and traffic is moving again. See you later, honey, probably in a couple of hours."

Casey nodded, leaning back against her pillow. She had a childish desire to be out walking through the snow, maybe even tossing a snowball. She sighed, dismissing that idea. It would be at least another week before she was released from the hospital.

"Hello."

Flipping her head toward the familiar voice, her heart almost stopped beating.

Steve was standing in the doorway, his dark hair ruffled by the wind, his lean face pale and haggard.

"Steve! Come in." Her surprise at seeing him sent the blood rushing to her cheeks. Her gaze flicked down his woolen overcoat and returned to his face, ruddy from the cold.

He walked across the room and stood staring down at her, the blue eyes pained and haunted.

"You will never, ever know what I've been through," he said.

She stared at him. "What do you mean?"

He turned to pull up a chair, then settled his long frame in it. "Martha heard about your accident over the local news. She tried to reach us in Vail but we were out on the slopes. When she finally got in touch with us, I was frantic with worry." He leaned forward, reaching for her hand, then covering it with both of his. "By that time, the storm had hit and the roads were closed. I tried to charter a plane, but they closed the runway, too." He shook his dark head hopelessly. "My phone calls to the hospital only added to my frustration. What little information I got merely made me wonder what was *really* going on. Finally, some considerate nurse took the time to assure me you were really going to be all right.''

He leaned down to press his lips to her hand. Staring at his bent head, all the love Casey felt for him rushed back. She longed to take him in her arms, reassure him. Then she remembered that he had left town without returning her phone call. While she was no longer angry about that, the possibility that their relationship was over kept her at arm's length.

"How is Brad?" she asked, forcing a cheerful note to her voice.

He lifted his head, looking deep into her golden brown eyes. "Worried. He loves you so much—almost as much as I."

"Steve, don't." She pulled her hand free and turned to face the window.

She couldn't bear to hear those words if she could never belong to him. She stared out the window at the snowy mountains, willing herself to be calm.

The silence lengthened. She heard him moving about and slowly turned back to face him. He was standing up again, removing his coat this time, and draping it over the chair.

Dressed in a tan ski sweater and dark slacks, he was as appealing as ever. *More* appealing, she thought, with the swift ache that comes from knowing something you want is forever out of reach.

"I suppose I should be thankful for the snowstorm," he smiled at her. "It proved a blessing. Brad and I were forced to stay at the condominium, even though I was wild to get back here to you. Brad made me realize a lot of things," he sighed, sinking into the chair again.

"What things?" she asked softly.

He paused, studying his hands. "He brought his

190

Bible along. When we first heard about your accident, the first thing he wanted to do was pray. When I called the hospital, I was told you were in Intensive Care—" he broke off, the blue gaze lifted to her face searchingly. "I knew then how much you meant to me, and how empty my life would be if . . ."

"Go on," she prompted.

"Then Brad and I prayed together," he said reverently, as if the idea were still almost too new to comprehend, too sacred to share. "Afterwards we read his Bible together. Amazing things began to happen there in the living room of our condominium. Brad and I were able to open our hearts to each other, and then," he reached for her hand, " as we began to pray for your recovery, I was filled with a quiet kind of peace. I knew you were going to be all right. *I knew it.* And after that," his blue eyes sought the distant mountain range, " I began to read the Bible again, searching for answers, for the kind of faith I've seen in your life."

He looked back at her, squeezing her hand gently.

"I found that peace, Casey. I gave my heart to Jesus and asked him to come into my life—to mend all the broken places, to make me a better person."

"You did?" Her eyes widened in surprise. "Oh, Steve. . . ." The words would not slip past the lump in her throat.

"Casey, there are some things I need to say to you, some things you need to understand. You are the only woman I've ever loved! As I told you, in matters of the heart I have no sense. Scarlett took my breath away in the beginning," he paused, the blue gaze never wavering from hers. "But soon after we were married, I realized I had never really known her. I fell for the outer beauty, without knowing the real person underneath."

He paused, choosing his words carefully. Casey

knew that he would not speak unkindly of Scarlett now, and she respected that. She would not voice her own opinions, either. Her conversation with Martha had disclosed the whole sad story.

"I think that became the source of all my guilt. I knew I didn't really love her. Working became an escape from that fact and," he sighed, "even from Scarlett herself. When she was sick, I kept thinking that I should take more time off to be with her, but I didn't. If anything, I worked harder!"

He shook his dark head, lost in some distant memory.

"Still, I would have done anything to save her. We called in the best doctors, flew her to special hospitals. But in the end there was nothing anyone could do. And she became so hard to live with! Maybe if I had loved her, I would have had the strength to stand up to her temper tantrums, or to administer her medicine reasonably. As it was, I merely gave in to her." His face was a mask of tragedy.

"Steve, I understand," Casey said quickly. "You don't have to say more if you don't want to . . ."

"I want to. Don't you understand? I'm free now." He studied her small face, strengthened by the love she saw in her eyes.

"That night she died, she threatened to take an overdose of medicine," he continued quietly. "She had made that statement so many times before that I finally quit protesting. I suppose I should have known that she would eventually carry out her threats. Yet, I always believed that they were just made to taunt me, to cause me pain. She made the usual threat that night as I was leaving her room. This time I just shrugged and walked out. I had heard it so many times before . . ." He lifted a hand, pressing long fingers to the taut muscles at the base of his skull.

"You shouldn't have tormented yourself for so long." Casey shook her head with regret.

They sat in silence, each considering the story he had told.

"After I came to know the kind of person you are, I didn't feel worthy of your love," he continued, his voice husky. "But I know now that I was merely taking the coward's way out. It was easier to run from the situation than to try to change it. Finally, you left me no choice," he leaned forward, touching his lips to hers.

She relished the feel of his lips, her heart overflowing with love for him. Then, remembering something, she pushed away, forcing him to look her in the eye.

"Why didn't you return my phone call?" she asked.

He sighed, a look of regret on his face.

"I picked up the phone to call you a dozen times, but I could never finish dialing the number. I kept thinking what a clean-cut guy that Walt Pennington was—that the two of you would have so much in common. I tried hard to convince myself that he might be a better man for you than I."

"Listen, Steve Simpson, I'm perfectly capable of picking my own friends! For your information, Walt Pennington is *not* my type."

"Well, it really deflated my ego when I came rushing over there to tell you something important, only to find you leaving the building with his arm around you!"

"What were you going to tell me?"

"After I lost that last case, I made up my mind to quit running from the truth."

"The truth?" she repeated, searching his face.

"I realized that my work was never going to fill the gap in my life. That I was so head-over-heels in love with you I might never win another case. I found myself reading the same paragraph in my legal books, over and over, never getting you out of my thoughts long enough to concentrate." For a moment, they sat staring at one another. "That was why I took off to Vail, hoping to clear my head, hoping to get over you. It didn't work." There was a long pause. "Well," he looked around the room, fragrant with the aroma of flowers, "all that is in the past. Do you realize that Christmas is only two days away? We need a tree." He was circling the room thoughtfully. "Some ornaments and lights. Maybe we'll even dangle a star from the ceiling. . . ."

"Steve, I don't think the nurses will go along with all that," she laughed. "I wouldn't mind having a tiny tree though, just something simple," she added wistfully.

"You'll have it! And we'll share the happiest Christmas ever right here in the hospital room. Then we're going to start the new year off right."

Casey looked at Steve, her memory drifting back to the day before when she had finally surrendered to God's will for her life. Was it possible that already God was blessing her with the desires of her heart? With Steve and Brad?

"Why so quiet?" he asked.

"Yesterday I was lying here looking out at the mountains, remembering our walk through the snow at Vail," she confessed. "I thought about what you said to me there, about my faith being as strong as a mountain—remember?"

"Of course I remember."

"There's a verse in Psalms that says 'Lord, by thy favor thou hast made my mountain to stand strong.' The mountain refer's to one's faith," she explained. "I've thought about that verse many times since. And I know my faith isn't nearly as staunch as that lovely mountain out there," she nodded her blond head

194

toward the towering peak. "But with each storm I do seem to grow stronger."

"Casey, I want that kind of faith, too. With your love and your help, we're going to make it. I really believe that now." He smiled down at her.

"I believe that, too." Her gaze slid over his shoulder to the window.

In the distance the morning sunlight haloed the crown of Pikes Peak, promising a dazzling winter day. Stunned by the beauty of the scene before her, she reached for Steve's hand. Suddenly she felt the strength of the mountain in the man beside her. With God's blessings they would build a mountain of faith and, like the mountain, their love would endure.

ABOUT THE AUTHOR

PEGGY DARTY, a former advertising and public relations copywriter, is now a full-time author whose works have been published by Bantam Books, *Parents Magazine, Lady's Circle, Home Life,* and others. She and her husband, Landon, reside in Jasper, Alabama with their three children.

It is Mrs. Darty's primary objective to present real-life characters who overcome obstacles through faith and love, and to inspire readers with the eternal significance of hope.

A Letter To Our Readers

Dear Reader:

Pioneering is an exhilarating experience, filled with opportunities for exploring new frontiers. The Zondervan Corporation is proud to be the first major publisher to launch a series of inspirational romances designed to inspire and uplift as well as to provide wholesome entertainment. In order that we might better contribute to your reading enjoyment, we would appreciate your taking a few minutes to respond to the following questions and return to:

> Anne Severance, Editor
> Serenade/Saga Books
> 749 Templeton Drive
> Nashville, Tennessee   37205

1. Did you enjoy reading A MOUNTAIN TO STAND STRONG?

   ☐ Very much. I would like to see more books by this author!
   ☐ Moderately
   ☐ I would have enjoyed it more if _____

2. Where did you purchase this book? _____

3. What influenced your decision to purchase this book?

   ☐ Cover   ☐ Back cover copy
   ☐ Title   ☐ Friends
   ☐ Publicity   ☐ Other _____

4. Please rate the following elements from 1 (poor) to 10 (superior):

☐ Heroine   ☐ Plot
☐ Hero   ☐ Inspirational theme
☐ Setting   ☐ Secondary characters

5. Which settings would you like to see in future Serenade/Serenata Books?

_____   _____

_____   _____

6. What are some inspirational themes you would like to see treated in future books?

_____   _____

_____   _____

7. Would you be interested in reading other Serenade/Serenata or Serenade/Saga Books?

☐ Very interested
☐ Moderately interested
☐ Not interested

8. Please indicate your age range:

☐ Under 18   ☐ 25–34   ☐ 46–55
☐ 18–24   ☐ 35–45   ☐ Over 55

9. Would you be interested in a Serenade book club? If so, please give us your name and address:

Name _____

Occupation _____

Address _____

City _____ State _____ Zip _____

Serenade Serenata Books are inspirational romances in contemporary settings, designed to bring you a joyful, heart-lifting reading experience.

Other books in this category, now available in your local bookstores:

#1 ON WINGS OF LOVE, Elaine L. Schulte
#2 LOVE'S SWEET PROMISE,
     Susan C. Feldhake
#3 FOR LOVE ALONE, Susan C. Feldhake
#4 LOVE'S LATE SPRING, Lydia Heermann
#5 IN COMES LOVE, Mab Graff Hoover
#6 FOUNTAIN OF LOVE, Velma S. Daniels and
     Peggy E. King
#7 MORNING SONG, Linda Herring

For lovers of historical romances, watch for *Serenade Saga Books*. The first six titles were available in February, 1984, and will be published alternately with *Serenade Serenata*, one title per month.

papers before her. "I'd like to go over some of the